HIDDEN

HIDDEN

Shelley Shepard Gray

AVON
INSPIRE

An Imprint of HarperCollinsPublishers

HarperCollins books may be purchased for educational, business, or sales promotional use. For information please write: Special Markets Department, HarperCollins Publishers, 10 East 53rd Street, New York, NY 10022.

HarperCollins®, 🌿®, and HarperOne™ are trademarks of HarperCollins Publishers.

FIRST EDITION

Interior text designed by Diahann Sturge

Library of Congress Cataloging-in-Publication Data
Gray, Shelley Shepard.
  Hidden / Shelley Shepard Gray.—1st ed.
    p. cm.
  ISBN 978-0-06-147445-3
1. Amish—Fiction. 2. Bed and breakfast accommodations—Fiction. 3. Abused women—Fiction. I. Title.
  PS3607.R3966H53 2008
  813'.6—dc22   2007045601

  09 10 11 12 ov/rrd 20 19 18 17 16 15 14 13 12 11

To Charlie and Cindy, Dale and Nancy, Cathy and Don and Janice. And Tom! Thank you for letting me learn from you, grow with you, and most of all . . . be myself.

Let anyone with ears to hear listen.

Mark 7:16

When the Holy Spirit comes to you, you will receive power. You will be my witnesses.

Acts 1:8

If you admire our faith—strengthen yours. If you admire our sense of commitment—deepen yours. If you admire our community spirit—build your own. If you admire the simple life—cut back. If you admire deep character and enduring values—live them yourself.

—*Small Farm Journal* (Summer 1993)

Prologue

Rob's right fist hurt more than she'd remembered. That was the first thing Anna thought as she tried to focus through the pain. Tried not to cry in front of him.

But that didn't stop Anna from cupping her palm protectively over her cheek, just in case Rob decided to hit her again.

Rob was sitting across from her once more, his crisp Brooks Brothers dress shirt hardly wrinkled. He scowled. "What, Anna? For once you have nothing to say?"

With a force of will, she dropped her hand and clasped her palms together. Resolved to stay calm. Yet, one more time, her mind played back to what she'd seen in his office earlier that day. How he'd been cashing checks for personal use from his campaign funds. And, worst of all, the realization that he'd spent some of that money on her. "There isn't anything to say. Not anymore."

"That, my dear, is where you're wrong. I don't ever want to hear that disbelieving, sarcastic tone in your voice again. And once more, you will never even think of mentioning your opinions about my business when we're in public again. Do you hear me?"

He was yelling. Of course she could hear him.

But now she believed his threats. After she'd questioned the receipts she'd found in front of one of his closest staff, Rob had been livid. Less than an hour later he pulled her out of the party, saying they had things to discuss. He'd barely spoken a word to her the whole way home. She had a feeling this was coming. And yet had hoped that his anger would subside, that it wouldn't come to this.

"Anna, answer."

"Yes." Unable to help herself, she nodded. The movement swayed the diamond drop earrings. When she'd first received them, she'd loved the sweet tinkling noise they made. Now that she realized they'd been bought with money from Rob's supporters, their weight merely intensified her piercing headache.

Rob's eyes followed the flash of the diamonds against the shadows of his living room wall. Anna knew the look that glinted in his eyes. It spoke of satisfaction. Ownership.

How had she been so very wrong about him?

Color returned to his cheeks as Rob leaned back against the cushions of the cream-colored couch. "Don't forget who you are talking to. We have a future together, Anna. We have plans."

She didn't even try to hide the bitterness in her voice. "I don't date men who hit me."

"That was an accident."

"Rob—"

His voice hardened. "It was an accident, Anna."

She knew it hadn't been. Instinctively, she knew he'd planned to hit her from the moment she said too much at the party. "Are you sure?"

Almost smiling, he raised his brows. "Come on. We both know I'm not the type of man who would hit a woman. But I'm also not the type of man to let a woman walk all over him. You need to learn your place, Anna. Learn your place and not forget it."

Unfortunately, she was slowly learning her place. She was just sorry it had taken her so long.

And that was the problem, wasn't it? Rob Peterson was all polished veneer. He was smooth talking, gift-giving, perfectly handsome and extremely well-mannered. When he'd first asked her out, Anna had been foolishly excited that he'd even noticed her.

And though he'd seemed possessive and at times controlling, she'd pretended it was only natural that a man like him would want everything to be perfect.

After all, he was running for a seat in the House of Representatives. He was an important man. A lot of people thought so.

As weeks turned to months, she'd quit her job and took another one—a silly position at an insurance company where she didn't have to work full time. Rob had asked that she'd be available at a moment's notice. To attend fundraisers and society galas.

When he took her shopping and paid cash for a closetful of designer dresses, skirts, and shoes, she'd pushed aside her own feelings for the clothes, even though she would have usually never worn skirts so form-fitting, necklines so low, or heels so high. After all, those things were important to Rob and the clothes were so much nicer than anything she'd ever owned.

But now Rob wasn't going to let her go. She knew it, and he knew it. Now her cheek knew it, too.

She was trapped.

As she sat across from him, felt his gaze on her, noticed that her cheek was swelling, Anna knew there was only one thing to do. She had to get away.

She tried to smile. Let him think she was just going to shrug this off as she had the other times. Standing up, she smoothed the jade green silk sheath around her hips. Stepped toward him on four inch heels. Close enough to smell his cologne.

Close enough for him to touch her again if he wanted to.

Tried to think of a lie he would believe. "I'm sorry about everything, Rob. I had no business saying a word about your finances, especially since I love your gifts so much. The truth is, I . . . I've been nervous about our future."

His dark brown eyes turned languid. "What are you nervous about?"

She picked a reason he would completely accept. "I saw how you were talking with that girl at the party earlier this evening. She was flirting with you nonstop."

"Who?" Rob leaned forward. Ran a finger up the expanse of her bare arm.

"The redhead?" Anna pretended to almost forget the woman's name. "Sammy?"

"Oh. That was *Samantha*, not Sammy." Oh, so gently, Rob pulled her down next to him. "Don't give her another thought. She's a nobody. You have nothing to be nervous about, baby. No other girl is like you. I get compliments on those pretty green eyes of yours almost every day."

Anna looked down so he wouldn't see the emotion she was trying so hard to conceal. But just as firmly, Rob tilted her chin up, so they were almost eye to eye. Almost tenderly, he wiped away a stray tear from her cheek. "Don't cry, Anna," he murmured, frowning. "I'm just doing what I have to do."

Inside, her nerves were warring. Fear and regret churned together, making her feel faint and nauseous. Anna knew she couldn't continue the charade much longer. "I think I better go home."

"Already?" He glanced at his gold watch. "It's not even midnight."

She tried to smile. "You're forgetting that I'm a working girl. They're expecting me at nine a.m. sharp." She pulled away and reached for her coat.

He followed her to the door. "As soon as we're engaged, you can quit," he murmured as he helped her slip on the black wool coat over her shoulders. After fastening the top button, he leaned closer and grazed his lips across her ear. "Then your time will be all mine."

Her heart was pounding. "I know it will. I'll see you tomorrow, Rob."

Just as he leaned close to kiss her, his cell phone rang. Looking at the screen, Rob grimaced. "I've got to get this, Anna. Sorry."

She slipped out.

There were twenty steps to the car. She just had to make it twenty steps. With every ounce of effort, Anna walked slowly, her back straight, her head high. Just as if Rob was watching from the window.

Ten more feet.

Two more. She slid into her sedan, turned on the ignition. Placed the car in reverse. Slowly edged the car down the driveway. Switched to drive. The front curtain fluttered as Rob finally walked away.

As she drove down his street, Anna dared to lock the doors. Safe. She was almost safe. The tears came, fast and furious. There was no doubt anymore, she had to get away.

Everyone loved Rob Peterson. They loved his smile, they loved his promises. Her parents thought his commanding manner was just what she needed. So far, no one had believed her when she tried to tell them he was dangerous. No one believed that he could hurt her, that he would hurt her. Especially not his brother-in-law, the sheriff.

Yes, as far as everyone was concerned, Anna Metzger already belonged to Rob Peterson.

With a ragged breath, Anna knew what she had to do. Before it was too late, she had to go someplace where no one could find her. She had to hide. By morning, she would have a plan. And then, to almost everyone who knew her . . . she would be gone.

Chapter 1

"Anna! This is surely a *gut*—a good—surprise," Katie Brenneman said in her all-too-familiar lilt. "Come in out of the cold, wouldja?"

Anna breathed a sigh of relief. For a moment she hadn't been sure she'd be welcomed by her childhood friend. Hadn't been sure of anything anymore.

Katie clucked. "Anna, come in. You're lettin' in the cold."

Obediently, she stepped into the foyer of the Brenneman Bed and Breakfast and was immediately surrounded by the smell of beeswax, spiced oranges, and crisp cotton. Behind her stood a finely woven basket filled with beautifully hand-carved canes of different woods. To her left was an antique table and chairs, each piece finely crafted and shined to a polish. A simple staircase curved upward to her right. Rag rugs in twirls of blue, dark green, and blood red decorated the wide planks.

On those planks, she placed her small suitcase. Well, maybe it wasn't so small.

Katie noticed. "You here for a spell?"

"I hope so. If you don't mind."

"Why ever would I mind?" Katie, dressed in her simple cobalt blue dress, gathered her into a warm hug, the kind of acceptance that only a friend of ten years could offer. "You're as cold as I've ever seen," she said, looking Anna up and down with bright blue eyes. "But something's wrong, ain't it now?"

Anna knew there was no way to sidestep her problems. Something was, indeed, very wrong. "I need help, Katie." Did her voice sound as desperate as she felt?

Katie's cheeks brightened with color, and she was just about to speak when Anna heard another voice, one that she'd tried hard to forget.

"Katie? Who's here?"

Anna turned to find Henry Brenneman filling the doorway, his expression guarded and full of distrust.

Katie stepped closer, as if her slight build could offer Anna protection from her brother's probing eyes. "It's Anna, my friend from *Mamm*'s quilting class, Henry."

"I see."

Anna was sure he did. From the time they'd first met, he'd always seemed to find her lacking.

Gesturing to her bulging suitcase, he said, "You here for a visit?"

Anna flushed. Against her will, she felt her composure falter. But that was always how Henry made her feel, unworthy. So . . . English. "Not exactly. Actually, I'm not sure why I'm here. I was just going to speak to Katie—"

His suspicious gaze cut her off as sharply as his words. "Why?"

Piercing brown eyes scanned her without embarrassment, leaving Anna to feel like the interloper she was. "I need somewhere to stay for a bit."

Katie motioned her silent with a finger to her lips. "We're due for a visit. I, for one, am delighted you're here. We have two bedrooms open. You're welcome to one, if you'd like."

"They're paying rooms."

Katie playfully pushed her brother's shoulder. "Get along, now. We'd never charge my *gut* friend Anna here for her company."

Anna stepped forward. Though it was kind of Katie to attempt to smooth over her appearance, Anna was done speaking—or acting—in veiled ways. "There's a reason I need a room."

Katie gripped her hand and pulled her into the kitchen, finally pressing Anna down into a wooden ladder-back chair. To Anna's dismay, Henry followed, though neither she nor Katie had invited him.

"I'm in trouble. I've been in trouble." Picking up the linen napkin on the table, Anna gently rubbed it against her cheek, doing her best not to wince as she did so. Little by little, the thick makeup she'd put on just a few hours ago came off, revealing her bruise.

Katie's eyes widened appreciatively. Henry, too, must have been struck by the discoloration under her cheek, because he sat down as well. Then, as was their way, neither said a word.

Anna remembered the wonderful sense of privacy that seemed to surround the Brennemans and their Amish relatives. Though part of the New Order, so not quite as strict in the ways of the Old, where electricity and modern conveniences were always forbidden, the Brenneman family adhered to many of the tenets of the Amish way of life—and that included an extreme respect for the privacy of others.

That respect made what had happened even more uncomfortable. "I . . . I should begin by letting you know that I've been dating Rob Peterson. For six months."

Blank expressions met the news.

They had to be the only people she knew who weren't fazed in the slightest about that. "He's kind of a famous man in Cincinnati. He's a former lawyer. Now he's running for the open spot in the House of Representatives." When still neither said anything, she added quietly, "He has a lot of influence. Money."

"And this matters to you, Anna?" Katie said.

Anna knew it didn't matter near as much as it used to, "Rob and I had already gotten serious when I started to notice how controlling he was. Prone to bursts of temper. The first time he hit me, he swore it was an accident."

"And that?" Henry asked.

She gingerly fingered her swollen cheek. Swallowed. "This happened late last night."

If anything, Henry's gaze hardened. "That there was no accident."

Henry was right. "No, no it wasn't. He, uh, now seems to think of me as a possession. He's taken to following me, or to having someone who works for him do that."

"Have you gotten the law involved?"

Anna almost smiled. Katie's knowledge of the outside world

was sketchy at best. "I've contacted the police, but they seem to think I'm just clumsy. No one wants to go against him."

"Not even your family?" Katie's voice was full of wonder.

For the moment, Anna had forgotten that her mother and Katie had formed a relationship. They'd gotten along very well, especially when Katie revealed that her cousins owned a dairy one hour north. Her mother claimed that the Amish products were the finest she'd ever had.

"My mother thinks I'm just having second thoughts about marrying Rob. She's always felt I didn't take anything very seriously."

Something flashed in Henry's eyes before he hid it—but Anna knew what he thought. It was the same thing everyone thought—there wasn't much to Anna Metzger. She'd made mediocre grades, had hardly ever kept a job more than six months, and had more than her fair share of boyfriends.

Her mother had plenty of examples of Anna not taking things seriously.

"So you've run?"

Henry's voice was full of accusation. But still, she couldn't deny it. "Yes. I ran."

"And in doing so you've put my family in danger?"

"No. I would never do that."

"But you did."

Anna sought to explain. "First, Rob doesn't even know about you. We didn't talk of things beyond his work and our social calendar." She paused before continuing. "Second, I'm sure I wasn't followed. I took a taxi here."

"But you canna be sure, can you?"

"No."

Henry folded his arms across his chest.

And made Anna realize she'd been a fool. Again. Scooting out her chair, she stood up quickly. "I'm sorry. I'll go."

Under her white cap, Katie's eyes were bright and questioning. "Where will you go?"

"I don't know."

"Maybe you shoulda thought—"

Katie turned to her brother. "Enough, Henry. Go tell *Mamm* and *Daed* that we have company, will ya?"

Henry put on the straw hat he'd been carrying and left without a word.

Next, Katie glanced at her. "Sit down. Now, I'll make you some tea, dear Anna, and you can tell me how else you've been hurt."

"There's not much else besides my cheek." *Not at the moment, anyway.*

"Inside though, I'm guessin' that will be another story."

Katie's eyes looked so caring that Anna almost broke down. "Oh, Katie, thank you for being here."

"Where else would I be? This is my home, *jah?*"

Anna sat still while Katie busied herself with a pot of tea, carefully spooning the loose leaves into a strainer and boiling the kettle on the kerosene stove.

Katie then carefully cut off a thick slice of apple bread and served it to Anna on a piece of oatmeal-colored crockery.

After her childhood friend seated herself again, Anna spoke. "I'm scared. I'm scared of Rob. And just as frightened to look in the mirror and truly see what I've become. *Whom* I've become. I never thought I'd be the kind of woman to hide from anyone."

"Sometimes we all hide. Even from ourselves. But, the Bible says we must seek shelter with the Lord."

"I suppose."

Katie bustled with the tea again, pouring and straining. With easy motions, she brought a jar of honey to the table. When she was settled again, she smiled. "Whatcha been doing, otherwise?"

Anna chuckled. "I've been working for an insurance company sometimes."

"And you like this?"

"No. I took it because the hours were flexible and I never had to get too emotionally involved. I could leave when I needed to help with the filing at campaign headquarters. Or when Rob wanted me to go out."

Katie blinked, telling Anna quite simply that she found the idea of being emotionally distant strange. "Will they be lookin' for you today?"

"I imagine so, though I did call and tell them I was taking some time off."

"I see," Katie said, though it was evident she didn't see at all.

"I spoke to my mother yesterday, but when all she did was laugh off my worries, I knew I had to leave. The disastrous episode with Rob late last night just confirmed I made the right decision. I purchased a plane ticket to Miami and parked my car at the airport. Then I left a message on my parents' home phone, saying that I was taking two weeks' vacation." With a shrug, Anna added, "I don't know if it will buy me much time, but I'm thinking it might."

"And then you came here."

"I went to the taxi stand and paid a small fortune for a ride out here. I truly didn't know where else to go."

Maybe because the Lord was guiding you?"

How could Anna describe completely the things she yearned for? Peace, tranquility. Faith and simplicity. Steadfast love. All were things the Brenneman family had shown her on numerous occasions over the years.

All were things that seemed to lie on the outskirts of her existence.

"You were right to come here, Anna."

"I don't think everyone feels that way."

"You talkin' bout Henry? He doesn't trust you."

There was the fact, said boldly and without rancor. "I know. Because I'm an Outsider?"

"Maybe. I think it might be something more, though," Katie said cryptically.

Mrs. Irene Brenneman entered just then, saving Anna from deciphering that message. "Anna, my dear. What a sight you are. Henry says you have need of shelter."

"Yes."

"Then you must stay here."

"If you're sure."

"Of course we're sure," she said, bending down and placing one soft cheek next to Anna's.

"I'd like to earn my keep. I can pay for my room and board and help out in any way I may."

"If you help, no money will be necessary," Irene said briskly. Turning to Henry, who was once again hovering near the door, she said, "Show Miss Anna to the room off the kitchen, would ya?"

After receiving a wink from Katie, Anna hastened to follow him, his hand already gripping her luggage.

"I can get that."

"It's no trouble."

She followed him down a wide hallway, the walls covered with a few carefully framed quilt squares. Anna recognized two of her favorite designs, the Bear Paw and the Monkey Wrench, the former icy white and indigo blue.

Finally, they stopped at the last room on the left.

"This is a small room," he warned.

"It will be fine."

He opened the door and set her bag just inside. "Well, then," he murmured. "I'll be seeing you, I suppose."

"Does my being here upset you?"

Instead of answering, he volleyed a question her way. "What would you do if it did? You arrived, bag in hand and marks to show. We didn't have much choice in the matter, now did we?"

"I didn't make up my circumstances."

"I didn't think you did." Finally he turned to her, his eyes piercing. "I think you're a selfish woman, Anna Metzger. I think you've chosen to run and hide and put my family in danger instead of facing your own consequences. And, I'm sorry, but I don't have much respect for that. My mother and sister have a soft spot for you, so I'll abide their wishes, but I don't like it."

"Thank you for your honesty."

"You're—welcome." With a last look before he shut the door, Henry added, "Honesty, I'm bettin', is something new for you."

Chapter 2

"I'm mighty disappointed in you, Henry," Katie said the moment he entered the hearth room in back of the kitchen. "The way you acted toward my friend Anna was terribly rude."

Henry fought to keep his expression neutral as he met the questioning looks from his sister and parents. He knew he'd been harsh and inhospitable toward Anna Metzger, but he hadn't been able to help himself.

Anna's appearance in his life had rattled him good. Not that his brash little sister needed to remind him of it. "I wasna being rude—only saying the truth. Which, I might add, is more than we are hearing from Anna."

Katie set her sewing to one side. "The bruise on her cheek looked mighty real to me."

Taking a seat in front of the blazing fire, Henry shook off

the cold look of his sister. "*Jah*, but I think there's more than what she's told us."

"I reckon there is," his father said as he peered at Henry through his reading glasses. "I fear there's far more to Anna's story than what she's shared with us."

"All the more reason to be circumspect, don'tcha think?"

After sharing a glance with his *daed*, his mother reached out and clasped his arm. "Oh, Henry. What has happened to you? You used to be far more accepting of others."

He spoke with more force than he intended. "Just because I don't immediately put my trust in an English girl who shows up for the first time in years doesna mean the problem lies with me."

"You couldn't have been any more discourteous, though." Katie picked up her sewing again, the bright yellow fabric shining bright against her dark skirts.

"Any ruder than arriving for a visit unannounced and uninvited?"

Most likely in a lather, Katie presented her shoulder to him while she spoke as sweet as molasses to their mother. "*Mamm*, thank you for allowing Anna to stay here."

"No reason to thank me, it's our Christian duty," her mother replied as she picked up the spool of thread that had just rolled off of Katie's skirts. "It's not our place to judge, Henry. Our Lord takes care of that just fine, without any help from us."

There, in the back room off the kitchen, one of the few rooms reserved only for family, Henry knew his mother was right, which made his cross feelings toward Anna even harder to understand. "I'll try to do better."

His father nodded and picked up his Bible. "I'm pleased to hear that."

Feeling too restless to remain seated by the fire, Henry stood up. "I'll go out now and check the horses."

"*Danke.*"

He'd just put on his black hat when his mother spoke again. "All women are not like Rachel, Henry."

Rachel. It was truly amazing, just how easily the woman's name could cause him grief. "I know that."

Katie's hands stilled. "Do you? Rachel was my friend once, too, you know. Sometimes I think you've forgotten."

He'd forgotten nothing. He'd been courting Rachel Baar for two months when she met an Englisher who was visiting the farmer's market. Lightning fast, Rachel left their community and married the man. Henry had watched, hurting but unable to do a thing to stop her journey into the outside world.

For many a day, he'd worked hard and long hours in the fields surrounding their inn . . . anything to divest himself of Rachel's memory and the hurt feelings she'd left him with.

He'd thought he'd accomplished his goal. He'd been sure of it until he saw Anna with her thick blond hair and bright green eyes at their doorstep.

Anna brought back memories of the first time he'd seen her, seven years before. Now, as before, he'd been struck by her beauty. "Rachel is not the problem here."

Katie raised her chin. "Neither is Anna."

"I don't agree. She should have sought shelter somewhere else. It is not our place to harbor her."

"She's my friend."

"She's English. And she could bring trouble with her. Maybe she already has."

"Henry. Katie. Quieten, now," their father ordered. "Your sharp tongues will lead you to trouble, mark my words."

Not ready to apologize yet again. Henry just nodded before slipping into the kitchen, then finally out into the bitterly cold January frost. Glad for the warmth of his thick wool coat, he made his way to the barn and their four horses. From the moment he entered his sanctuary, Henry felt right once again. Stanley raised his head in Henry's direction, neighing a friendly greeting.

From the back room, Jess carefully padded forward. Kneeling down, he took time to rub his old dog behind the ears. "Jess? How are you, my friend?" Warm brown eyes softened with trust as a fluffy brown and white tail wagged. "Did you eat? Let's go see."

Jess stepped alongside him, walking to his water and food bowls, which were still full. After taking a sip of water, Jess sat down on his favorite blanket and watched Henry with bright eyes. That Jess wasn't eating made him sad—there'd been a time when the dog would sneak bacon and pancakes from the kitchen counter with lightning speed.

Now Jess preferred the quiet of the barn and days filled with sleeping.

Henry sank to the dog's side and leaned his back against the rough wood of the barn.

Just for a moment, he remembered the past. Remembered how he'd always assumed things would be.

Rachel.

From the time he sat next to Rachel in their one-room schoolhouse, Henry had known he'd found his heart's match. Rachel had been everything he'd ever wanted.

Though nothing had been said, Henry—and everyone

they knew—had assumed that when Rachel turned of age, they'd marry.

But she'd cast her eye on another man and left everything she knew with little more than a backward glance.

And now he was faced with the only other woman who'd captured his attention, and she was everything he shouldn't want. An outsider. Far more educated than he. Far more worldly than he.

Her hair, so full of curls, so thick and pretty it captured his imagination from the time he'd seen it hanging down her back in a loose ponytail. Green eyes, so sharp and filled with expression that every emotion was written plain on her face. A bright smile. Creamy skin.

And never more than a cursory glance his way.

Over the course of the late January afternoon, the Brenneman Bed and Breakfast filled, leaving Anna no time to discuss things further with Katie or her mother.

Instead, she kept herself occupied in the kitchen, carefully rolling out dough for the evening's batch of apple dumplings.

First thing that morning, Mrs. Brenneman had handed her a simple blue dress, woolen stockings, and a crisp apron, offering it to Anna as a way of keeping the rest of the guests from observing her too carefully. Anna had gratefully slipped and pinned on the garments, appreciating how the well-worn cloth felt against her skin and kept her warm.

Voices, loud and boisterous and foreign, filled the inn's halls. Anna hid a smile as she overheard Katie discussing the nearby general store with a couple from Tennessee. Over and over, Katie patiently answered their questions concerning the Amish way of life.

When Katie entered the kitchen again, Anna raised an eyebrow in her direction. "All those questions! Do they ever bother you?"

Her friend looked surprised at the thought. "Oh, not at all. People come here to be a part of our way of life. Given that, there's always questions."

"Sometimes it seems too intrusive."

"If we found it such, we wouldn't open our home," she replied softly.

Anna stewed on that as she carefully brushed a layer of butter on the top of each cloverleaf roll that she'd just fashioned into the tin. "I know you're right."

"I am."

"I'm sorry I've taken up a room. I'm costing you money, I'm afraid."

"You're important, too, Anna. You mustn't forget that."

Anna ducked her head, realizing with some surprise that she was carrying that sense of unworthiness from Rob. "I'll do my best to be helpful. Just tell me what to do and I'll do it."

Katie gently touched her cheek. "If you do your best to heal, that will be enough."

"The mark isn't so bad."

"We both know better, Anna. The mark is a symbol of many bad things."

Anna's hands shook as Katie was summoned out of the kitchen. Katie's words were very true. Her relationship with Rob had been unhealthy from the very first—she'd just never been strong enough to see that.

No, that wasn't true. She'd hadn't been strong enough to take control of her life and change things. But now, she was slowly changing and determined to use the time at the

Brennemans to grow both spiritually and in maturity. Though living with the Amish was proving to be full of long days and hard physical labor, for the first time in her life, Anna wasn't afraid to commit.

It truly seemed as if her friendship with Katie and the Brennemans' hospitality was a gift from God. Anna just hoped she wasn't destined to hurt the very people who were giving her aid in the process.

She frowned, thinking about the outside world. What was happening at home? With Rob?

Did he even realize she was gone? A number of scenarios ran together in her head. Rob knowing immediately that she never left the area. Rob searching through her belongings and finding some careless note that Anna had scrawled on a scratch sheet of paper.

Rob coming out to the Brennemans and reclaiming her . . . and she going with him because she had no choice.

No matter what Henry said, she wouldn't put the Brennemans in danger. She owed them too much. Was too appreciative of their kindness to her.

But what if she already had?

Digging her hands into the dough once more, Anna prayed.

"Florida? Are you sure she flew to Miami?"

Meredith Metzger clutched the phone, biting back the sharp worry that engulfed her as she scanned her daughter's note again. "Rob, that's what she said. Anna also left me her itinerary. She decided to go with some girlfriends to the beach for two weeks. Don't worry."

"Who are these girlfriends?"

"Jennifer and Linda," Meredith said, making up two names from the top of her head.

"I've never heard of them."

Taking care to put the right amount of amusement in her voice, Meredith chuckled. "Rob, please don't tell me that you and Anna spent your time together talking about her long list of friends."

"This trip seems sudden. Too sudden."

"Maybe it wasn't," she ventured. "Now that I think about it, I believe Anna had this trip planned for months and I just forgot about it." Doing her best to keep the conversation light and easy, Meredith laughed. "That sounds like Anna, doesn't it? The girl would forget her hands if they weren't attached to her arms."

"Maybe you're right," Rob said after a moment, his usually silky voice sounding stilted and rough. "Though that doesn't explain why she hasn't answered her cell phone. Every time I call, it just rings before going to voice mail."

"She's probably just not taking it to the beach with her."

"Maybe. When you talk to Anna, tell her to call me. She should have never left without contacting me first."

True worry settled in Meredith's heart. Had the man always been so controlling and she'd just been blinded by his wealth and good looks? "I'll do that, but I doubt she'll call home today." Summoning a girlish, artificial laugh, Meredith said, "You know how Anna is—always out for a good time."

Still no humor infused his voice. "Tell her to call me as soon as you do—no matter what the time."

After she hung up, Meredith stared at Anna's hastily scrawled note one more time.

Mother,

I'm going to Miami for a few weeks. Sorry I forgot to tell you about it earlier. I'll call you in a few days.

Anna

No matter what Meredith told Rob, taking a trip on the spur of the moment was not like her daughter. Neither was forgetting about it.

Something wasn't quite right.

Meredith quickly climbed the staircase to her daughter's room. Lifting up the powder blue dust ruffle, she noticed all of Anna's suitcases were still neatly stowed under her bed.

Pulling open a drawer, she saw it was filled with shorts and bathing suits—too many if Anna had really packed for a trip in the sun.

She investigated further. Sunscreen was in the medicine cabinet in the bathroom. Sandals rested on her closet floor. Her camera sat on her dresser.

No, something wasn't right at all.

Neither was Rob's anger.

Foreboding filled Meredith as she wondered if maybe—just maybe—her daughter might not have been exaggerating when she said that Rob Peterson was a dangerous man.

"Please be with her, Heavenly Father," she prayed. "Heaven knows I have not."

Chapter 3

The air was icy cold and its breeze bit into her cheeks as Anna crossed the well-worn path from the main house to the barn where the horses were stabled.

And where Henry Brenneman had seemed to be more often than not. Hearing the clang of his hammer, Anna wondered if he was still as angry with her as he'd been the evening before. She certainly hoped not. The last thing she'd meant to do when she'd sought refuge at the inn was cause distress.

Her steps faltered. Who was she kidding? She hadn't thought of anyone but herself during that hour-long trip from the airport to the Brennemans'. In many ways, Henry's accusations were not far off the mark.

After knocking on his closed workshop door, she called out, "Henry? Your mother wants you in for breakfast."

After a moment's pause, the workshop door opened. "I'll be right out."

For a moment, Anna couldn't help but stare. Henry's cheeks were flushed from exertion, and his sleeves were rolled up. Beads of sweat dotted his brow and neck. Under a worn leather apron, broad shoulders and an iron-hard chest peeked out. Henry Brenneman was gorgeous.

How had she not noticed that before?

It took her a moment to remember to close her mouth. "You're working out here awfully early."

He almost smiled. "Me and Jess here do best in the morning," he said, gesturing to the old dog sprawled on what looked to be a discarded horse blanket.

She peeked in further, smelled leather and wood oil, dust and horse and . . . Henry? She swallowed. "What are you working on?"

"Only a chair that needed fixin'." As if her proximity made him nervous, he took a step away, broke eye contact. "As I said, I'll just be a moment."

Anna nodded, and took a step back as well, lengthening the distance between them. Though a little voice inside her said she might as well turn and leave, Anna decided to wait for him. She needed to make some kind of peace with Henry, if for no other reason than to ease the tension in the Brenneman household.

With easy motions, Henry untied his apron, righted the chair, and put each tool in its proper place. Anna watched him with something close to surprise, as if she'd just seen him for the first time.

Why was that? How had she never noticed how handsome he was? How steady? How much he cared for that old dog? Had she only been concerned with herself?

Or had she only thought of him with a label firmly attached? Amish. Foreign. Different. All the tags she'd never pinned on Katie.

As if surprised she was still there, he frowned. "Tell *Mamm* I'll be right along."

Offering an olive branch, she said, "I'll wait for you, if you don't mind."

"*Danke.*" Wariness filled his brown-eyed gaze.

Anna leaned against the doorframe as Henry knelt down to Jess and gently patted the dog behind his floppy ears. He whispered something to him, then straightened and met her at the barn door, resolution in his eyes.

As their boots crunched over the fallen leaves and stones underfoot, Anna offered, "Will your dog be okay out here?"

"*Jah.* He's happy as long as he can stay put here."

The cold air made her eyes water. "You've had him a long time?"

"Thirteen years. Long ago he used to keep me company when I worked in the fields."

"Now Jess has earned his retirement."

Once again, Henry almost smiled. "Retirement? We Amish don't believe in such things."

Anna wasn't sure if he was teasing or not. "You just slow down?"

"We follow God's will, Anna Metzger. That's what we do."

Anna stewed on that as Henry held the door open for her and they stepped inside the bustling kitchen.

"There you both are," Mrs. Brenneman said, holding a platter full of eggs and sausage. "I thought I was going to have to send Katie out for you, mark my words."

As Henry sent a superior look Katie's way he said, "It's lucky we came when we did, then."

After a moment of silent prayer, Henry started eating. Anna served herself a smaller portion while she stewed on Henry's abrupt change in manner.

She mentioned it to Katie later when they were clearing the table and preparing for the guests, who would start coming down for breakfast at seven thirty. "I don't understand your brother. One moment, he seems angry at me for everything I've done, the next, he seems almost sociable. I hardly know how to act around him."

Katie chuckled. "It's because you make him nervous, Anna."

"Me? I don't see why."

Mrs. Brenneman stirred her coffee. "Don't fret, my dear. He'll find his way."

Find his way around what? Her? "Do I make him nervous because I'm English?" That didn't make sense. Most all the guests in the bed and breakfast were English, weren't they?

Katie chuckled. "You make him uneasy because you're *Anna*."

"What is that supposed to mean?"

"We've all caught him sneaking a glance your way a time or two over the years when you've come visiting," Katie explained, her eyes twinkling.

Anna felt her cheeks heat. "I had no idea."

Mrs. Brenneman clucked. "That almost makes it harder, I think. My *buwe*, my son, is having a time of it, preparing for his future. His Rachel fell in *lieb* with an Englisher and left us all. Your appearance brings back memories."

"Makes Henry think of things that are not possible—at least not for him," Katie added matter-of-factly. "He's made it really clear he has no need to live outside of our ways."

"And here I was, pushing him to accept me. I'm sorry."

"Nothing to be sorry for," Mrs. Brenneman said with a warm smile. "You being here is wonderful *gut*."

"Thank you."

Katie's mom clapped her hands. "Now, dear, you did a fine job on the rolls yesterday, but I have a different chore for you this morning, if you've got a mind for it."

"What is it?"

"Sewing."

Sewing and quilting were two of Anna's favorite pastimes. So much so, it didn't seem like work. "Wouldn't you rather I did something more helpful? I'd be happy to help clean the guestrooms."

After pulling out a finely woven basket filled with indigo cloth and white linen from a cupboard near the kitchen door, Mrs. Brenneman placed it in front of Anna. "This chore would be most helpful, if you don't mind doing it. I've cut the cloth for a new shirt for Henry and a new dress for my eldest daughter's baby. If you could work on them, I'd be mighty happy."

With a kind smile, Katie added, "The sewing room is in the back and has a nice rocking chair and fire. With the morning light, it's a peaceful place."

Looking at the platters of food still needing to be washed, and the plates of muffins to serve to the guests, Anna still worried. Though she'd come to hide, she certainly didn't want to shirk the many jobs that needed to be done. "If that's what you would like me to do . . ."

"I would," Mrs. Brenneman said, gently cupping Anna's sore cheek. "Today's a time for resting. Tomorrow's soon enough for more."

"I'll join you after I finish helping the guests get organized for the day and washing the walls and floor of the kitchen," Katie promised.

"I'd be happy to sew, Mrs. Brenneman. But first could I help with the dishes?"

"Yes, dear Anna. First, you may help with the dishes."

The day had been fulfilling in a way that working at the insurance company had never been. After helping with the dishes, Anna carried the sewing basket into the back room and inspected the fabrics for the dress and shirt. Both cloths were finely made and soft as the finest materials in expensive department stores.

Luckily for Anna, there were also patterns to follow. In no time, Anna was working at the trundle sewing machine stationed in the corner of the room. Time flew as she painstakingly pieced the garments together.

After a time, Katie joined her for a bit, then left when it was time to prepare two of the rooms for new guests. Anna helped with some baking, then went to her room to prepare for the evening meal.

As she approached her room, the discordant sound of her cell phone interrupted the quiet tranquility of the house. Quickly, she hurried to her room and had just picked it up when Mr. Brenneman loomed in her doorway.

He eyed the small silver phone with distrust. "Anna?"

"I'm sorry, I didn't know this was on."

"If you're planning to stay here a length of time, I trust you'll think twice about using your electronics." Waving a hand at her dress and cap he added, "Especially seeing as you are hoping to blend in."

"I'm sorry, I forgot to turn it off." After quickly seeing she had two missed calls, Anna ignored the temptation to check to see who had contacted her. Instead, she quickly pushed the power button and turned off her last link to the outside world. In seconds, the screen went black. "It's off, now. I won't use it again while I'm here."

"I thank you for that."

"If you don't mind, I'd be obliged if you'd take this," she said, handing Mr. Brenneman the thin silver phone.

He balanced it on his palm as if it were about to explode in his very hand. "That isna' necessary. It is enough that you give me your word."

"I know, but I want to earn your trust."

"It's not my trust we should be concerned about, Anna. When all is said and done, it's all really about us and God, don't you know? Our personal relationship with Him and His word is what matters."

Our personal relationship. How funny that her childish faith had fled to the background as she'd stepped farther and farther into the brash culture of Rob's place in society. "I'm sure you are right. But if you don't mind, I'd still appreciate you putting that phone away. I don't want to be tempted to use it or to leave just yet."

Mr. Brenneman looked alarmed. "Truly, Anna? You'd go back to a man who so terribly hurt you?"

"I don't think I would, but I can't always trust myself anymore," she said softly, thinking about how topsy-turvy her emotions had been lately. "I'm afraid if I speak to my mother, she might convince me to return, and I'm just not sure if that's the right thing to do."

"I see." As if that settled the matter, Mr. Brenneman closed his hand around the phone and slipped it into the deep front pocket of his heavy wool shirt. "I'll put this away for a time, for safekeeping, but it's always yours, Anna."

"*Danke*, Mr. Brenneman."

Her awkward pronunciation brought a true smile to her host's lips. "You're welcome, dear Anna."

When she was alone again, Anna wondered what would have to occur to prompt her to ask for the cell phone back. Something very good . . . or very bad.

Hands shaking, Meredith Metzger watched Rob pull his Mercedes away from the curb and speed away. When he was out of sight, she pulled the blinds down tight and sat on the couch, doing her best to ignore the urge for a cigarette.

"You okay, dear?"

"No. Calvin, I'm scared to death. Rob was nearly violent."

Sitting down beside her, her husband rested his hands on his thighs. "Nearly? Rob 'nearly' tore Anna's room up and took a box full of her personal items to examine. I 'nearly' called the cops."

Linda swallowed hard as her eyes pricked with tears. "That wouldn't have helped, would it?"

"No. Anna said she'd called the police before and all they did was advise her to calm herself. Between Rob's prestigious family connections and his current office as county commissioner, I don't think there's a person here in Ohio who would easily think ill of him."

"We did the same thing two weeks ago. She told us how worried she was about Rob's controlling ways."

"I know." With bleak eyes, Calvin said, "She wanted to break up with Rob."

"And I told her she was throwing her life away."

"How could we know things were different? To our defense, our daughter was never one to hold onto a commitment."

"Not even a little bit. Three colleges."

Calvin held up two hands. "Seven jobs, last time I counted."

"At least that many 'serious' boyfriends. Oh, Calvin, Lord help me, but I thought she needed discipline."

"We can't blame ourselves for seeing Rob's heavy-handed ways as nothing more than a way to encourage her to grow up."

"And now she's out there. Somewhere. I hope she's okay."

One more time Calvin picked up the phone and punched in Anna's cell phone number. Meredith watched anxiously. When he frowned and hung up, she leaned forward. "What happened? Why didn't you leave a message?"

"This time I didn't even hear a ring. Either her phone's been turned off or its service has been disconnected. Meredith, I hate to admit it, but I'm afraid we have to face the truth. Anna's gone."

Closing her eyes, Meredith prayed for her daughter's safety and health. And that wherever she was, she was well and hidden from Rob.

Otherwise, Meredith was afraid that even the Lord wouldn't be able to save her from the man's temper.

Chapter 4

The voice reverberated through the near empty office suite, clattering in Rob Peterson's head and making it pound.

"Rob, you need to forget about that girl and get back on target. We're charging two hundred a head for the dinner tonight. For that kind of cash, people are going to expect their money's worth."

Rob looked hard at Bill Williams, his campaign manager and right-hand man, and wondered why he'd ever thought he was worth the salary he was paying him. "Don't pressure me."

Bill lifted his head in surprise, before returning his concentration to what he did best—shuffling folders. Bill always organized folders like a gigantic deck of cards, his hands in motion. The nervous gesture betrayed his jovial oh-gosh-oh-gee way of speaking. "Don't pressure you? Rob, you pay me to me to pressure you."

"The dinner will be fine. I'll do what I always do, tell them what they want to hear."

"These people are a little savvier than that, Rob. They're going to want to know what you plan to achieve as their new representative. This is the big time. The majors, you know? A whole different ball game."

Bill had always enjoyed over-stating the obvious. At the moment, he was getting on Rob's last nerve. "Stop the whining, Williams. I've never not done what is expected of me."

"You have recently. You were late for the luncheon at the women's club."

That had been because he'd stayed too long at the Metzgers', looking through everything and anything to find a hint of where Anna had gone.

He'd found nothing. The box he'd eagerly removed from the Metzgers' only contained patterns for quilts, maps, and notes about the Amish, of all people.

Who knew Anna had even thought of such nonsense?

His irritation at the Metzgers had almost caused him to lose control when they had stood at the door, as if they were attempting to fend him off.

It had taken everything he had not to grab Meredith Metzger and shake the information out of her. She had to know where Anna was. Had to.

Because he needed Anna back. *Nobody left him.*

Nobody made a fool of him.

"Rob, are you even listening to me?" Bill's voice turned whiny and loud, burning deep and annoyingly shrill.

He'd had enough. With almost more force than he intended, Rob slammed his hand on the desk. "Don't question me again. If you're not careful, you won't have a job."

"Sorry, Rob." Bill's eyes widened and his hands stilled for a split second. His face paled enough that Rob felt a burst of satisfaction rise through him. Satisfaction, and the niggling disappointment that the only thing that ever seemed to work was the hint of retribution.

It had been that way with Anna time and again. She'd only become obedient after a reminder of his power. Only then would she look at him with respect, with fear and submission.

It was a shame mere words never seemed to work.

When Bill still looked at him warily, Rob did his best to shift his expression into something close to patience. "Did you bring me notes about the attendees?"

Bill deposited a folder in front of him. "I did. It's mainly going to be a bunch of bigwigs from the north side of town." Grinning broadly, Bill added, "Get this, they believe a portion of the dinner will be benefiting the Leukemia Society."

"Ah, yes. One of my favorite causes."

Bill chuckled. "They're all your favorites, Rob."

That was true. Long ago he'd learned to do and say anything to get his way. As he opened the folder and began to skim through the selection of notes written out for him, Rob's mind drifted back to Anna. Anna, with her perfect figure and green eyes. Her full lips and bright, easy smile.

Everyone loved Anna. People noticed him more when she was there. Looked at him with respect, like he must be something special if a girl like that wanted to be by his side.

He needed her back. He needed her in his life. Maybe he should hire an investigator?

"Rob, about the—"

"Go away, Bill. I don't need you right now."

Relief floated through him when the front door opened and shut, finally allowing Rob to sit with only the silence of his thoughts for company.

"You're up even earlier than usual," Anna said after she got dressed and sleepily wandered into the kitchen. The morning sun had yet to make a bit of an appearance, but already Katie looked neat and pretty, her cap securely pinned on, and a black apron over her pale blue cotton dress.

"I'm going to the general store today," Katie announced. "We need supplies."

Something about the way Katie was talking about the store made Anna take a second look. "*That's* why you're so excited? Because you're in a hurry to purchase flour?"

"And for other things, maybe."

Before Anna could comment on that, her friend poured them two cups of coffee and spoke again. "I'm helping *Mamm* today with washing and ironing, so I thought I'd get some of that done early. Would you care to help?"

"I'll be happy to. What would you like me to do?"

"Begin the ironing?"

"I can do that. I'll go heat up the irons."

"*Danke.*"

Though Anna had watched Katie or Mrs. Brenneman iron many a time before, their calm, cool manner made the chore seem easier than Anna found it to be. Anna felt ironing in their kitchen to be anything but easy. The heated irons were heavy and hard to get used to, and the heat emanating from them made the hair on her forehead curl even more than it usually did.

But she was diligent, and before she knew it, Anna was

carefully smoothing fabric over the ironing board, taking her time to smooth out the wrinkles from the cotton fabrics that had dried on the clothesline near the hearth room. By her side, Katie maneuvered the fabric with practiced ease, having no trouble judging the temperature of each iron.

After Anna finished her third shirt, Katie broke the quiet. "I must tell ya, Anna, you have surprised me."

"How? That I haven't scorched a shirt yet?"

"Maybe. Also the way you are adapting to life here." She set the iron down. "I've always thought of you as a fancy girl."

Anna would have described herself much the same way. Well, maybe not "fancy," but spoiled and used to her conveniences. And, no wonder. Most people no longer ever thought twice about where their power came from, going to the giant supercenters or considered the untold electronics they assumed they needed just to prepare for the day.

Here at the Brenneman Bed and Breakfast, life was much slower. And though there was electricity for the guests' sake, the Brennemans, by and large, took little advantage of it.

As she hung another shirt on a wooden hanger, Anna said, "I never would have thought I'd be happy right now, but in some ways I am. I appreciate the silence, and the lengthy time it takes to do things I once hardly realized I was doing."

"You'll accompany us tomorrow for our services?"

"If your parents don't mind, I will."

"*Mamm* and *Daed* will be happy to have you with us, for sure." With a sweet smile, she added, "We're going to the Kringles'. My sister Rebekeh will be there with her family. I canna hardly wait."

"It's been a while since you've seen her, hasn't it?"

"Almost six months. Too long."

They worked in silence for a while longer.

"What makes you so excited to go to the store today? Is there someone you'd like to see?

Twin spots of color decorated her cheeks. "No."

"Oh, okay."

Like a child, Katie stepped forward, words bursting through her. "Well, if you must know, there's a man I some-times see at McClusky's."

"Who's that?"

"Jonathan Lundy."

"Have you known him long?"

"Not so long." Peeking around the kitchen, Katie lowered her voice. "As a matter of fact, we don't know each other too well at all. But he's a widower, has two daughters, and he lives on a farm not far from here. One time we spoke."

"Ah." Anna struggled to keep wistfulness from her voice. Contrary to what Katie might have thought, Anna didn't find her friend's fascination with Jonathan Lundy silly at all. Instead, she felt more than a little bit jealous.

It had been quite some time since she'd been a part of something so innocent and pure, something opposite of her life with Rob. When had she last felt infatuation? In high school with Mark, her first "real" boyfriend? Just thinking of Mark and the butterflies she used to feel around him made her smile. All he'd had to do was smile for her heart to pound.

But then he'd found someone else, and she'd become jaded. Her love life had slowly spiraled downward until she'd ended up with Rob.

His toxic demeanor and way of looking at life had poi-soned the rest of her innocence. Now, she sometimes felt incapable of seeing the best in people. She instead wondered what they wanted, why they did the things they did.

"One Saturday, three months ago, Jonathan asked how my family was."

"And you said?"

"We are well."

"Sounds like an appropriate response." Anna could picture it now, Katie with the elusive Jonathan Lundy, both too shy to say more than a few words to each other in greeting.

When was the last time she'd felt like that?

"I suppose. Jonathan's wife was taken to the Lord a year ago July."

"That had to be hard."

"*Jah*. I'm afraid he needs a new wife."

"Why are you afraid? Is he mean?"

"Oh my goodness, no." Shyly Katie focused once more on her ironing. "I just fear that any wife will do, you know?"

"You're worried about being just a replacement."

"*Jah*. Maybe if I do catch his eye, it will be only because I can care for his daughters, not because he fancies a life with me."

"He'd never see you like that. No one in their right mind would."

"I don't know. Well, no use counting chickens, as they say." Clasping her hands on the edge of her apron, Katie said, "Please don't tell anyone about this. I'd be so embarrassed if Henry found out."

"I would never share your secret, especially not with your older brother," Anna said. Reaching out, she squeezed Katie's hand. "Thanks for trusting me with your secret. And, who knows—maybe everything will work out. You just have to believe in yourself, Katie."

"Well, right now, I believe I'm needed here at home. The Lord will guide me with Jonathan, I suppose. His timing is always right. And, in truth, Jonathan Lundy and I hardly know each other."

"I hope it works out," Anna said, carefully slipping an apron on yet another hanger just as Mrs. Brenneman entered the kitchen, her familiar smile lighting the room, though it was barely six in the morning.

"Anna, Katie, how industrious you two are today."

"Yes, *Mamm*. Just getting some chores done before we go to town."

"Who's going to take you?"

"Henry will when he's done taking care of the horses and Jess."

Anna turned to Katie in surprise. For some reason, she'd thought the two of them would go by themselves.

Katie explained. "Henry said he had a few things to get as well."

Irene pointed to a neatly written note on the counter near the back door. "I've written a list down, don't forget. Oh, and I've another chore for you both, while you're out and about. I want you to deliver some bread to the Lundys."

Katie's eyes grew into saucers. "Really?"

Anna kept her eyes on her iron so she wouldn't be tempted to share a smile with Mrs. Brenneman. If Anna wasn't mistaken, Katie's mother knew exactly who her daughter had a fondness for—secret or no secret.

"Really. Jonathan's sister Winnie is in town, don't you

know. She won't be able to come to services tomorrow, but I wrote her and told her I'd let her try my cherry bread and pass on the recipe."

"Sometimes Jonathan is at the store when we go. We might see him there," Katie said.

"Wherever you see him is fine," Mrs. Brenneman said easily before pulling out a cast-iron skillet. "Now we best get a hot breakfast ready for our guests. Otherwise, they'll be wondering what they're paying for."

Three of them in the open buggy was a snug fit. Henry glanced again at Anna Metzger and wondered why she was accompanying them, anyway. Wasn't she supposed to be hiding from the English?

Now, here she was, dressed Plain, and accompanying them just like she had every right to.

She was also looking at his horse Stanley with something akin to worry. "Will he be okay? It's a big load, the three of us."

"Stanley's a workhorse, not a lapdog. He could carry your weight or even more without taxing his strength."

Katie playfully nudged her brother. "Oh, Henry, you always say the wrong thing. You're supposed to tell us that with our light weight, we're no trouble at all."

Henry felt his cheeks burn as he realized his sister was right. He didn't have any soft words or coy remarks inside of him. Instead, all practicality ran in his head, leaving no room for sweet phrases or flattery.

Maybe that was why Rachel had left his side without a moment for looking back? Because he'd never done much to keep her close?

"I hope it doesna rain," he muttered.

"I hope it doesn't, either. We'll get soaked."

They moved along the old road, only having to move aside for a few cars.

Half an hour later, they arrived at the store. Katie and Anna clambered out of the buggy easily.

"I'm going to leave the bread here, just in case we don't see Mr. Lundy in the store."

Henry nodded absently as he guided Stanley to the side of the tall clapboard building and hooked up the buggy to a small hitching post. Then, he nodded to a few friends who were unloading carts of finely made toys before entering the McClusky General Store.

"Henry, good to see you," Sam McClusky said in greeting from the back of the store. Once a successful salesman, Sam gave it all up about ten years ago when he longed for a simpler life, one where he could spend more time with his children. Now he owned the store and ran it exceptionally well. Mennonites, Amish, and English all frequented the vast building, mingling with each other with the ease of years of practice.

"*Gut* to see you, too."

"You need something special?"

"I need some nails and a package of sandpaper, but I can take care of finding what I need."

"Very good."

As Sam went back to his business, Henry scanned the aisles, then found Katie chatting with a lady near two large quilts.

Where was Anna?

Finally, he did spy her . . . sitting by herself, looking pale and uncomfortable as a family of tourists stared at her and pointed. For the first time since she'd arrived a week before, Henry allowed himself to feel for Anna. The girl was in a difficult predicament; that was for sure.

Stepping closer, he pointed to the door. "Would you like to wait outside?"

"You don't mind?"

"I don't. Let me just tell Sam to charge my account for this." When he returned, she looked extremely grateful.

"Thanks so much," she said, already walking to his side. She stayed uncomfortably close as they wound their way through the narrow aisles and stacks of goods. "Leaving your home wasn't a good idea, I'm afraid. There are too many people here."

After telling Katie that she could take her time, Henry fought against his better judgment but lost as he walked Anna down the grassy hill to a set of picnic tables.

Luckily, the morning's clouds had passed and no rain was in sight. Instead, the cold, brisk air held a hint of sunshine, encouraging him to breathe deep and catch a taste of spring.

Turning to him, she smiled. "Thank you, Henry. I really needed rescuing back there."

"It was no trouble."

"All right . . . but no matter what, you escorting me out here is certainly appreciated."

For a moment, Henry let himself meet her eyes, felt the warmth of her gaze burn through him. Let himself imagine that she wasn't English and that he'd never heard of Rachel Baar.

And for that split second, with the sun shining and Anna

Metzger looking so fresh and pretty, Henry almost felt content. Hopeful.

But then, as she turned away and he spied the yellowish-purple remains of the bruise on her cheek, Henry knew that contentment was just as false as the paint she'd worn on her face . . . fleeting and covering up what they knew to be true.

Chapter 5

There was something in Henry's eyes that made Anna turn away. As she did, a rabbit hopped into the clearing and grabbed her attention.

Henry smiled with pleasure when she pointed it out.

After wiggling its ears fretfully for a bit, the rabbit settled in and relaxed. Doing much what she and Henry were attempting to do—enjoy a clear blue sky and wan rays of sunshine on an otherwise very cold day.

Seeing how Henry's brusque manner had finally softened, Anna dared to smile at him. "You have a way with animals, don't you?"

Henry shrugged. "I don't know if I do or not. I just appreciate them, maybe. All Amish do."

"Why is that?"

"The Amish believe we are as a part of our God's creation

as the berries on the trees, or this rabbit here. It's why we take such care to work the land, why we excel at work in the dairy, why we treat our horses like lifelong companions. It's what we've always done."

The pride in his voice made Anna realize that she'd struck a chord with him, and a good one at that. "The only times I've been to Amish country was to see Katie, and we talked mainly of quilting and the inn. I realize now that I've never thought about your work outside in the fields."

Henry's gaze remained on the rabbit. Almost like he was afraid to meet her eyes. "No reason you should," he mumbled.

"Well, I appreciate it now."

"Because it's cold outside?"

"Because I'm realizing that being outside with nature is where you were meant to be."

"I'm glad, then." Slowly, he added, "If you ever care to learn more about the hills and such around the inn, I'd be willing to share what I know with you. I've spent many an hour of free time walking in the woods near our home, enjoying the peace and quiet. "

"I'm trying to imagine your mother letting you do such a thing. You are a very industrious family."

"Work is not a burden."

His voice had hardened. The rabbit's ears trembled and Anna felt herself stiffen as well. Obviously, no matter how pleasant Henry was trying to be, he still didn't think much of her work ethic. "I didn't mean anything negative by what I said. I meant it as a compliment."

Henry waited a long moment, his body almost motionless

as the rabbit hopped a little closer, its nose twitching nervously. "I didn't take your words to heart, Anna. As a matter of fact, I wasn't thinking of you, I was remembering me as a boy." Miraculously, a red stain appeared on Henry's neck. "When I was younger, I'm afraid that I did have a tendency to wander a bit too much. It was in my nature, I suppose. Sometimes, not in my best interest or my family's."

The idea of the strong, steady man beside her dodging responsibility made her smile. "You? Goofing off?"

"I didn't do that. But sometimes maybe I took too long when it could have been completed fast, in half the time."

"Such as?"

Henry frowned. "Weeding my mother's garden. My sister Rebekeh always fussed, saying I took too long because I was studying the bumble bees or some such thing."

"Your stories always make me wish I had more family."

"Are you an only child?"

"I am, but not by my parents' choice," Anna said, realizing with some surprise she was finding it so easy to speak with Henry. "My mother was diagnosed with cancer soon after I was born. Though she had a complete recovery, she and my dad decided against any more children."

"So you grew up alone and afraid you'd lose her?"

His directness took her off guard. That, and the way he'd pinpointed her worries in a way that hardly anyone ever had before. "Alone, yes. Afraid, sometimes." Nudging a rock down the hill, she added, "I was terribly afraid the cancer would come back."

"But it didn't?"

"No. Well, it hasn't yet."

Henry swallowed. "I must admit I've been guilty of imagining your life and thinking that it had been too easy, soft. I was sure you'd never known hardship, had never concerned yourself with things that mattered."

"My life was different than yours, but not perfect. And not completely aimless, either."

"I'm realizing that now, as we've gotten better acquainted. When Katie would talk to us about you, after a visit, or a phone call, or a quilting class, I never thought about anything other than how different your life was. How fancy your clothes were, how fast and free your existence was. Even during my running around year, I never did the things Katie said you did."

Stung, Anna stared at her feet. "I don't know what you think I've done, but I promise you that my life hasn't been as full of sin as you make it sound."

A hint of a grin lined his mouth. "Let me finish, now, wouldja? What I'm trying to say is, I felt that no matter how much I might know or learn about you, I was sure that we'd have too many differences to ever have a friendship. I thought our differences would prevent a connection."

Henry's honesty, as always, made Anna wish she'd learned to hold her tongue a bit more. "I've done the same thing," she finally admitted. Stealing a look his way, Anna slowly added, "But now I'm coming to the conclusion that maybe we have more in common than I had previously thought."

"Maybe we do, Anna."

A rush of voices filled the parking lot behind them, making the rabbit freeze in midmotion, then scurry away. A mere rustle in the bushes was the only clue it had been there at all. In spite of herself, Anna held her breath, waiting for the rabbit to reappear—even though she knew it was silly to wish for such a thing.

"And now you're here. With us."

"Now I am." As more voices carried on the wind, Anna felt yet another burst of apprehension. Wariness engulfed her. Caution made her want to shrink and hide. Just like the hare, maybe if she was motionless, no one would see her, or guess where she'd come from.

But despite her attempts to blend in, she still stood out. Her posture was wrong, her eyes too aware. Fingering her dress, she whispered, "Henry, I shouldn't have left the inn. Seeing everyone here, both the Amish and the English, it makes me nervous. I feel like I don't look Amish enough, that I'm catching everyone's attention."

He'd noticed other men and women looking at Anna, but Henry felt it most likely had to do with the fact that she was a stranger, not an imposter.

But her nervousness made him curious. "If you're so sure you don't look 'right,' why did you want to come, then? To get away from your chores for a bit?"

After all they'd just said, did Henry still see her as a nuisance, nothing more than a lazy woman with a multitude of sins? "I was thinking of Katie, if you want to know the truth."

"Katie?"

Anna wasn't sure how much to share. "She was hoping to see some people she knew, and when I agreed, I thought it would just be the two of us going together. I knew she needed the company."

Henry's open expression shuttered and a soft look of

amusement flicked across his face. "People she knew, hmm? Well, now I understand."

Anna doubted it. But if he did, she sure hoped she hadn't given too much away.

"No matter," Henry said. "I or my parents should've thought those things through. It isna wise for you to be here—it opens up the world to too many questions." Looking behind him, Henry stood up. "My sister's done with her business now. Perhaps we should go deliver the bread and return. I've work to do."

"I think that sounds like a good idea," Anna said as Katie approached, though she couldn't prevent a certain amount of frostiness from peeking out. Henry could be so maddening.

Looking from one to the other, Katie frowned. "Have you two been arguing again?"

"No. Just talking," Anna said.

"Oh. Well, then." She cleared her throat. "Jonathan Lundy wasna in the store. I suppose we'll have to deliver the bread to his homestead."

Anna fought to hide her smile. Thank goodness Katie didn't have dreams of being on the stage, because her acting left a lot to be desired. Her voice sounded wistful and surprised, all at the same time.

Henry, on the other hand, scowled. "Are you sure that cherry bread has to be delivered today? The Lundy farm is five miles beyond our place."

"I am. *Mamm* asked us to deliver it, Henry," Katie replied as they walked up the hill and each took a box of supplies and loaded them into the back compartment of the buggy.

When that was done, Anna and Katie stood to the side while Henry checked Stanley's bridle and the buggy's hitch with steady, confident motions. Finally, he gestured for Anna and Katie to climb in. "I still think it's a waste of time, I'll tell you that. We'll see him at church tomorrow."

"It would be rude to hand him a loaf of bread to carry around all afternoon."

"He could put it in his buggy. That's what we are doing today, after all."

Katie frowned. "Henry, stop being so cross."

"I'm not cross; I'm just reminding you two that I have other things that need doing besides taking you on fool's errands."

"This errand is not foolish at all. Besides, *Mamm* asked us to do this." With an exaggerated sigh, she said, "Why Henry, you're acting as if this was my idea."

Henry opened his mouth, like he was tempted to say something about that. After a second, he pursed his lips and stared obstinately forward. Silence followed.

While Katie looked to be either stewing about her brother or eagerly anticipating their arrival to the Lundy homestead, Anna felt a different set of emotions wash through her.

They were leaving the crowded confines of the store. She felt safer, more hidden.

But by her side was a man who had almost seemed like he could be a friend . . . but instead had closed up again. She felt uneasy around him again and a slight disproval emanating from his posture.

It was like their conversation on the bank of the creek had never happened; the feelings of friendship that had begun to spring forth abandoned.

Old worries and the vague feeling of not ever fitting in surged forth, capping her earlier optimism.

Reminding her that she was getting no less than she deserved. One day she really needed to learn to stop trusting people.

"I'm going crazy just waiting to hear something, Calvin," Meredith said on Saturday afternoon.

As had become their habit, the two of them were standing in their daughter's room, looking at Anna's wide array of photos on her desk and wondering if anyone in them was their clue to Anna's whereabouts.

"There's not much we can do. Maybe Anna really did pack a bag and leave for Miami."

"I'm going to call some of her girlfriends and see what they say."

"Do what you feel is necessary, but I have to tell you, I think you're rushing things. We may be overreacting."

"You don't think it's strange that we haven't heard from her?"

"I do think it's strange, but not completely unheard of. She's a twenty-four-year-old woman, not a teenager on spring break. She doesn't need to call us every night."

"Calvin, you are deliberately being difficult."

"And you are deliberately forgetting that everything between our daughter and us is not all right."

She knew he was right. But that didn't mean she was wrong. "Things weren't that bad."

"They might be. Remember, we had quite a few words with Anna the night before she left. She may be in a snit. She may be even angrier than that."

Meredith sank to the edge of her daughter's bed and felt as if she would never forget that last conversation. Anna had been frightened and asked for help. Instead of listening and offering advice, she had done the complete opposite. Yep, while Anna had sat there, stunned, Meredith had pointed out every flaw in her daughter's life.

No, she hadn't forgotten a single one, had she?

Meredith had mentioned the price of college tuition wasted on degrees never earned. On interview suits bought for jobs that had lasted barely a month. Of lost opportunities with men who wanted a steady companion because Anna kept protesting those men—a long line of successful and attractive men—weren't special enough for her.

Anna hadn't thought she could love any of them.

Meredith's temper had snapped. She'd said almost unforgivable things, even going so far as to give her daughter a timeline. Told her it was time to grow up and take charge of her life and move out. That she and Calvin had had enough of her foolishness.

Anna had stared like she'd been slapped.

Then, the very next day, her dear daughter was gone. Crossing the room, Meredith walked to the desk and stared at Anna's note once again.

Mother.

When had Anna ever called her "Mother"? It had always been "Mom."

Only "Mother" when she was really angry.

Only "Momma" when she was really upset and scared.

Opening the top drawer of the antique cherry desk they'd given her on her seventeenth birthday, Meredith decided to hunt for a clue. Anything was better than just sitting and waiting.

"You sure you want to do this, Meredith? Anna won't like you going through her things."

"I need to find her address book. She needs me to get involved."

"Rob probably took everything of value."

"Not this." Meredith pulled out a spiral notebook. Underneath lay an old address book, the outside pale pink and decorated with purple stars, the edges frayed. She'd bought a new one in tan leather for Anna just last Christmas, but Anna had said she didn't want to transfer all the names and addresses. Not yet.

She'd thought it was yet another example of Anna not wanting to give up her childhood. "I'm going to start calling everyone, to see if they know anything. To see if she told them about her plans."

Calvin placed a reassuring hand on her shoulder, the warmth of his easy comfort sustaining her and giving her peace. "You sure about this?" he questioned again. "If we discover something and Rob finds out that we kept it from him, he could make things worse for Anna."

"Or us. That man obviously has no problem hurting anyone or anything standing in the way of his wants." When her voice started to crack, she paused for a moment to gather strength. And strength was what she needed—strength to continue in the midst of guilt and lost opportunities.

Strength to accept guilt and responsibility but to soldier on instead of hiding in the shadows.

Calvin placed a reassuring hand on her shoulder. "There might be another way. We can call the police again."

"We can do that, but I don't feel that it will do as much good. Besides, I need to do something besides wring my hands and wish I could do things over again."

"This isn't all our fault, Meredith. Anna has had a history

of being impulsive and not thinking things through. There've been plenty of times in the past when stepping into her business has helped her a lot."

"I know."

Calvin continued. "And, we didn't find Rob and make her date him. The two were in a very real relationship by the time we met him. Anna told me she thought she was in love."

"I know, but I'm slowly learning not to look at our daughter's life in plain black and white. No, Anna's problems are not our fault, but they aren't all hers, either. Something could have happened to her, something far worse than we could ever imagine."

"We'll pray and call, then."

"That does sound like the most reasonable option. We don't have a choice, do we?" Meredith picked up the address book, and clutched it to her chest as they exited Anna's room, then headed downstairs to the kitchen. "She may already be worse off than we can ever imagine."

Calvin filled the kettle with water, then handed her the phone and a pad of paper. "If she comes home next week with a tan and a smile—"

"I'm going to hold her close and be the happiest mother in the world."

Calvin laughed. "Go to work, then."

Meredith didn't laugh much two hours later. No one had heard from Anna. Most hadn't spoken to—or even e-mailed—her in months. That was surprising. Anna had always had a large circle of friends and appreciated a tight, long-lasting bond with them for years.

When Meredith had conveyed her surprise to Julie Gowan, Anna's good friend for years, Julie wasted no time mincing words. "It wasn't my fault, Mrs. Metzger. After I met Anna and Rob one evening for pizza, Anna called me the next day on the verge of tears. Rob had forbidden Anna to see me."

"What?"

"I felt the same way," Julie said wryly. "Rob didn't like my look. He didn't like my pierced nose, my tattoo, or my job."

"But you do so much good!" Meredith said, amazed. Julie's job at a halfway house for troubled teens was something to be proud of. "Anyone would be honored to know you."

"Not Rob. He was afraid somehow someone would sneak a photo of me and Anna together and connect it with him."

Hands shaking, Meredith tried to make sense of it all . . . but there was no sense—none whatsoever. "I don't know what to say."

"There's nothing you can say. Rob's refusal to look beyond my tattoos didn't bother me, Mrs. Metzger . . . I mean he didn't know me from any other person off the street. And, well, if you want to know the truth, I didn't care for him any more than he did me. But that Anna didn't even think twice about moving on? That hurt. I mean, we went to kindergarten together."

Resisting the impulse to apologize to Julie for her daughter's behavior, Meredith murmured, "I'm beginning to realize that there were a lot of things that happened with Anna and Rob that I didn't know about."

After a long pause, Julie said, "Look, I've been pretty upset with her for a while, but I'd never wish anything bad to happen to her. Tell Annie to call me if she wants to, would you? No matter what, I'm still there for her."

Meredith smiled at the old nickname. "I promise I'll pass on your message."

After she hung up, Meredith shook her head in wonder as she shared the story with Calvin. "I never thought I'd see the day when Anna and Julie weren't friends."

"Did Julie say she understood?"

"Julie said that she understood why Anna was doing what she had to do . . . and that she'd always be there for her. No matter what."

Tears filled Meredith's eyes for what had to be the hundredth time in a week. "Why didn't I say those things, Calvin? Why didn't I share my love with her more openly? Why didn't I ever make sure she realized that no matter what our differences, I would always be there for her?"

Instead of answering her, Calvin squeezed her shoulder. "You're only on 'G,' dear. You've got a whole alphabet of people to ask about Anna. Don't give up."

"I have fought a good fight, I have finished my course, I have kept the faith." The Bible verse from Second Timothy floated to her, giving her strength.

Chapter 6

"Do you think I was too bold around Jonathan Lundy?" Katie asked Anna three days later. They'd spent most of the day on the second floor, washing walls and dusting furniture until it gleamed.

Now they were in the attic guest room, cleaning it top to bottom in preparation for the next pair of guests, scheduled to arrive before supper.

"I don't think you were bold at all," Anna stated as she flicked a crisp cotton sheet onto the down-filled feather bed covering the mattress. "In fact, I don't think you said very much to Mr. Lundy at all."

"I spoke to him about the weather."

Anna conceded that. "And you asked if his daughters were happy with their teacher."

Katie nodded, her dust rag hanging limply. "Those are reasonable questions, don't you think?"

"They *were* reasonable," Anna said dryly. "I don't think they could have been any more reasonable."

Not catching Anna's slight teasing, Katie stewed some more. "I hope he didn't think me too forward. I'd be sorely embarrassed if Jonathan thought I was being too personal." Her eyes widened, shining blue like the pansies around the barn in the summer. "What if he thought I was hinting?"

Katie had lost her. "Hinting about what?"

"About his home life, of course. And his personal wants and needs. I mustn't act like I know he needs help." Katie swiped the windowsill, then turned to Anna again. "Should I?"

"I'm the wrong person to ask. Every relationship I've had has ended badly." And every relationship probably could have used a little more of Katie's thoughtfulness and consideration, too, Anna thought. Maybe then she wouldn't have drifted alone and lost for so long. Maybe then she wouldn't have ended up with Rob.

Together they unfolded the vibrant quilt that Mrs. Brenneman had hung on the clothesline during the stretch of sunshine that afternoon. Anna caught the scent of fresh air as they smoothed it onto the feather bed, the bright white, velvety violet, and indigo blue Ocean Wave pattern turning the otherwise spare room into one of beauty.

As she fluffed two pillows and carefully set them on top of the quilt, Katie ventured, "So you no longer care for your Rob Peterson?"

"No." She was puzzled by his actions, wary of what he might do next, and frightened of what would happen when they did meet again.

"*Daed* said you asked him to hold onto your phone, just in case you thought about returning to Rob."

"A few days ago I was afraid I'd give in. Now I feel stronger and surer of myself. It would also be true to say that he wasn't the only thing I'm hoping to hide from at the moment. I also need a break from my job and my life. I need time."

"Even from your family?"

"I love my parents, but we don't have the close bond you all do here. Plus, I haven't been as mature as I could've been this past year. Sometimes I think I've reverted back to fourteen again, only thinking about my hair and appearances," Anna admitted, remembering how concerned she'd been about looking "just right" by Rob's side.

"And then Rob hurt you."

"That tells you just how mixed up my priorities have been, don't you think? The Bible speaks often about honoring and caring for your friends and enemies. Lately I've been putting my trust in false idols . . . in money and privilege and things that don't mean anything." Pressing a palm to her cheek which was now void of any discolorations, Anna added, "I guess we could say I've learned from my foolishness."

"Do you really feel you deserved Rob's marks of anger? Surely you're not shouldering all the blame?"

Anna speculated that she hadn't been shouldering enough responsibility. She'd been charmed by Rob Peterson, even knowing that the things he believed in weren't things to be proud of. She'd encouraged his attention, even when her conscience told her she would regret leading him on.

And her conscience had been right. If she hadn't been mesmerized by Rob, she wouldn't be hiding from him now.

No longer could Anna wish things were different. The truth was, she'd been impressed with Rob's money, affluence, and power. When she'd been in his company, she'd allowed herself to forget what was important, what really mattered.

"I've made a mess of things in my life—my hiding here is certainly evidence of that. But right now, everything feels so overwhelming. I don't know how to fix anything."

Katie's concerned expression turned confident. "With prayer, of course."

"I've been praying." With some surprise, Anna added, "I know He listened, because here I am with you."

A look of sheer happiness floated over Katie's expression. One of innocence and love, pure and all-encompassing.

Had she only prayed for protection? "I have been praying for safety. I think I need to expand my goals. I need guidance, don't you think?"

With a soft laugh, Katie reached for her hand and clasped it. "Oh, Anna. Haven't you felt His guidance all along?"

Anna was prevented from replying when a door opened and slammed shut down below. *"Mamm? Daed!?"* someone shouted.

"That's Henry," Katie said with a start. Quickly, they left the guest room and started down two flights of stairs.

Below, Henry continued to yell for help. "Katie? Are you here?"

"I'm here!" she called out as she skipped down the stairs. Anna followed her closely. As if they were in jeans and tennis shoes instead of barefoot and clad in long dresses and aprons, they tore down one flight of steps, then another.

Anna barely caught her breath when they finally skidded to a stop.

"Henry?" Katie called out again.

"Here."

Anna felt as if her heart had stopped when they finally came face-to-face with Henry. Cheeks pale, eyes red rimmed, he was visibly doing his best not to cry.

"Henry, whatever's wrong?" Katie asked, running to his side.

After catching his breath, he replied. "It's Jess. He . . . he's dead."

Katie's face crumbled as a single tear fell from Henry's eyes. Without a word, she wrapped her arms around him. Henry hugged his sister close, burying his face in her shoulder.

Anna stood by the doorway, reeling from the news. With some surprise, she realized that she, too, would grieve for the dog she'd only seen a few times.

And then it hit her—the pain she felt was for Henry. Because he loved that dog. Because he was hurting. Because she felt helpless.

Irene came in. "Whatever is going on here? Henry and Katie, you two know better than to cause such a ruckus."

Anna spoke quietly. "Henry just found Jess—he's dead."

Pure sympathy entered her blue eyes. "Oh, now. That is a terrible shame. God bless that dog. Henry, what happened?"

Henry raised his head. After wiping his eyes with the corner of his fist, he said, "I don't know. I went to the barn to finish working on the chair and saw that Jess hadn't eaten. I thought he was asleep and reached down to wake him up." Henry's face became carefully blank. "That's when I knew that something was wrong."

"He was an old dog, Henry. He's lucky to have passed his way where he was happiest, in the barn on his blanket."

Katie nodded. "He was a *gut* dog."

"He was a *gut* friend." Looking almost embarrassed by the expanse of emotion, Henry glanced at Anna before leaving out the back door. For a long moment, only the echo of the whoosh of the screen door filled the kitchen.

"Poor Henry," Katie finally said softly. "He loved that dog. And Jess loved him."

"Jess was hurting." Irene laid a hand on her daughter's shoulder. "It was his time."

Spying Henry walking resolutely to the barn through the kitchen window, Anna asked, "What's going to happen now? What's Henry going to do?"

"He'll most likely decide where to bury Jess," Irene said. Walking to the window, she, too, gazed through the thick pane. "Perhaps Henry will choose the back field. Jess always did fancy the rabbits that nested there."

Anna realized that Katie and Mrs. Brenneman were prepared to let Henry take care of Jess all by himself. And Henry was prepared to do that as well.

Anna's stomach clenched as she realized she couldn't let him do that. She couldn't let him be alone. "Mrs. Brenneman, I'd like to help."

"With what?"

"Bury Jess."

"Oh, dear, you mustn't fret so. Henry will shoulder this burden without complaint."

But Anna didn't want him to have to carry that load on his own. "I'd like to help so Henry won't have to be alone."

"There's no shame in mourning a creature of God, Anna. Henry will do just fine."

Words failed her as she tried to make them see that she needed to be there for Henry. Needed it in a way she hadn't needed anything in quite some time. "Would you mind if I went to the barn?"

"I don' mind, but Henry may not want you there."

"I'd rather he sees me and refuses my offer than for him to think I didn't care. Please, Mrs. Brenneman, may I go to him?"

"Of course."

Anna was halfway to the barn before she realized that Katie had been conspicuously silent, only looking at Anna with a new understanding in her blue eyes.

Why?

Henry had wrapped Jess in the blanket she'd seen the dog lay on and had placed him in a wagon. He was holding a shovel and pulling on gloves when she entered.

With a jerky movement, he looked up. "Did you need something?"

"I thought I'd offer my help."

Henry looked genuinely puzzled. "With what?"

"I . . . I wanted to walk with you when you buried Jess."

She thought he was going to refuse. However, after a long moment, he nodded. *"Danke."*

She removed the shovel from his hands and hooked her cape securely around her as they walked out into the elements. Beside her, Henry pulled the old wooden wagon, the wheels creaking, signaling their unaccustomed use.

As the wind blew into their faces, they turned left and walked slowly onto the worn path, through a maze of fields that had been tended by the Brennemans for generations.

A sense of peace flew through Anna as they plodded along. For the first time, she felt Henry's longing for things to be different.

Maybe Henry's stalwart temperament didn't always serve him well. Maybe he wished he could sometimes ask for help or admit to disappointment and grief.

Their path grew steep. With a grunt, Henry adjusted his grip and lifted his arms a bit higher, easing his load, though Anna sensed it was not too heavy for him to bear.

The cold air bit into her cheeks, making her grateful for the black bonnet on her head. The brim shielded her face from the worst of the wind, and the thick woolen cloth helped to keep her head warm.

Finally they reached a thicket of woods. A few rocks and stones jutted out, keeping company with the maple and oak trees. A sharp scent of pine floated closer, making Anna think of Christmas.

Henry carefully set the wagon to rights. "This'll do, I think," he said softly, clearing a small spot of leaves.

Anna passed the shovel, then watched him use his foot to help pushed the blade into the hard, frozen earth and scoop out a patch of dirt.

Again, he dug, doing the same thing for almost an hour, removing his coat as the hole got bigger and deeper. Finally it was big enough.

Tears pricked Anna's eyes as she saw a wave of emotion fill his gaze as he bent to pick up the dog. His hands trembled for a moment before his arms braced to hold the load. Anna rushed to his side and supported a little of Jess's weight.

Together, they knelt and placed the dog's body in the earth. Anna was amazed at how small it seemed now.

"Would you like me to recite a psalm?"

Henry shook his head. "No. The Lord knows Jess was a good companion to me. I will miss him."

Yet, Anna was sure he still did say a prayer. Unabashedly, a tear tracked his cheek as he briefly closed his eyes. A moment later, he stood and picked up the shovel again. Anna pulled it from his grasp. "Let me," she whispered.

Amazingly, Henry complied.

Anna carefully set the first clump back in the ground, her heart breaking for Henry with each scoop. After a bit, Henry finished the job. And, when everything was back in place, he stepped back.

Around them, the woods seemed to come alive. In the distance, a jay squawked, closer a trio of branches rustled from the breeze. Overhead, the clouds broke, and a slim ray of sunshine filtered through, offering a band of warmth.

Henry cleared his throat. "I don't know why you came, but I thank you."

"You're welcome." Afraid to contemplate exactly why she'd had to be by his side, she held out her hand. To her relief and surprise, Henry clasped it right away.

The touch was combustible. A pulse beat through them, an awareness that had nothing to do with their differences and everything to do with a change in their relationship.

His face lifted, capturing her expression.

Then Anna knew what she had to do . . . she stepped into his arms and hugged him. Henry's arms folded around her, holding her tight.

His chin rested on the top of her head, and she placed her cheek on his chest. Even as she sought to comfort him, it was impossible not to be aware of how finely toned his torso was.

Of his scent. Of how warm and secure he made her feel on such a cold day.

Later, as Henry's shoulders shook and he dared to cry, Anna rubbed his back, as she would a small child, and murmured that everything was going to be all right.

Rob Peterson almost lost control at five o'clock that afternoon. It took every bit of willpower to keep his expression impassive as his sister's husband, a country bumpkin sheriff, spoke in circles yet again. The man's meandering statements and refusal to stay on topic reminded Rob exactly why he'd usually done everything he could to stay away from him. Axel Grant was maddening.

Irritated beyond belief, Rob interrupted him again. "What do you mean there's no way to check to see if Anna is in Amish country?"

"I mean if she's staying at someone's house, most likely, we wouldn't know it." His brother-in-law shifted a wad of chew from one side of his mouth to the other. "Most don't have phones, you know."

That was inconceivable. "How do they communicate?"

Axel dared to smile. "The old-fashioned way—they talk face-to-face."

"And in emergencies?"

"Some folks do have phones that they share with neighbors. We could try to track down some of them, but it's going to be like looking for a needle in a haystack."

Grant was a real fan of clichés.

As the sheriff spit into the plastic cup he was holding, worry coursed through Rob as he imagined the things that Anna would be telling strangers. His misuse of campaign contributions. The times his temper had gotten the best of him. He needed to find her before she spoke to someone who actually cared, who actually would do something with the filth she would most likely be spewing about him.

If he lost the election, he'd lose more than just a job. He'd lose his power.

Where had he gone wrong with her, anyhow? When they'd first met, she'd seemed so impressionable and dim. She'd taken his gifts easily enough, slipping on the diamond earrings the moment he'd handed them to her.

Smiling brightly when he'd placed the heart locket around her neck. She hadn't done more than blink when he'd glided a finger along the smooth skin of her collarbone after fastening the chain of gold around her neck.

She'd gone into his arms easily enough after that. In fact, she'd been so pliable, Anna had never done anything but what he'd asked her to.

Until he'd lost control and hit her.

It was then that everything changed and she began to question him more. Every so often, she'd not look pleased to see him when he picked her up at the insurance company.

Once she almost refused to help him answer the phones when his office had been particularly busy.

And it was then that the light seemed to go out of her eyes whenever he touched her. He'd known how she acted—like she was only putting up with him. Dealing with him.

Suffering through his advances. Her genuine love for him had turned and become fake and full of lies.

He'd hated the changes. And hated that it was almost too late to claim her. And he'd intended to do that, no matter what.

He'd dreamed of her. Buying her clothes, showing her off, having other men look at him in envy.

Now she was about to remove herself from his grasp and ruin his reputation. It wouldn't be tolerated.

"Where is this area? I'll go there myself."

"I'm telling you now, don't expect to see a bunch of Amish standing around in the middle of the road, congregating. They've got things to do, I tell you. Why, they're the busiest folks I know, from sunup to sundown." Resting a scuffed, dirty boot on his opposite knee, Grant nodded complacently. "Yep, those Amish are real hard workers."

Rob glared. He hadn't asked for the Amish daily schedule. *When would people ever learn to listen to him?* "Axel, I need information, not advice. Please."

Stung, Axel looked at him with widening eyes. "If I was you, I'd go to the Brenneman Bed and Breakfast. You can use that as a home base for a few days while you look around."

Like he was going to spend the night with some backward hillbillies. "I can't take that much time off."

"Then I suggest you wait a bit. Your woman most likely got cold feet, and decided to assert a little independence. Don't fret, she'll come back to her man . . . they always do."

The reminder of ownership made Rob almost happy. "You think so?"

"I know so." His brother-in-law plopped both feet back on the ground. "In the meantime, you might want to go take a spell at McClusky's hardware. If they've seen your blonde, they'll let you know." Pointing to the professional photograph Rob had taken of Anna just the month before, he said, "A girl like that will stand out anywhere."

"I hope you're right."

"I do, too, Rob. I do, too." Replacing his hat, Axel left, leaving Rob with too many questions and no way to get answers.

When the phone on his desk started ringing and no one was there to answer it but him, a wave of frustration hit him hard. Rob cursed again. Anna was such a disappointment.

As was his infatuation with her.

The phone rang again. "Peterson," he barked. "Oh, sorry, William," he tempered his voice as he realized that one of his bigger campaign contributors was on the line. "I just burned my hand on the coffee pot."

"You, pouring coffee?" William Scott's laughter came through loud and clear from his end of the line. "There hasn't been a time we've met when you haven't had someone standing around you, seeing to your needs."

Rob struggled to keep his voice calm and steady. Light. "I do all right on my own, William. It would be a sad state of affairs if I couldn't handle even the simplest of chores."

"I'll second that. Where's that pretty girl you had in your office last time I visited? She made us a good pot of coffee. Seemed to me you two were getting along just fine."

"Anna stepped out for a moment, but she'll be back soon. I can promise you that."

"The two of you still courting, then?"

Rob winced at the ancient language. "We are."

"Good. I've spoken to quite a few people on your behalf, Rob. We like you—and are ready to do whatever it takes to see that you're elected."

"I appreciate that."

"I'm glad you do. I must warn you, however, that a great majority of the folks I've talked to are a mite concerned about your bachelor status."

The old man sounded more blustery with every conversation. Rob struggled to keep his patience. "I'm not the first bachelor to hold office, William."

"That may be true, but we'd like to see you looking more like a family man." He paused. "As a matter of fact, everyone likes the sound of that woman I told them about. What was her name, Amy?"

"Anna. Her name is *Anna*."

"Ah, yes. Let me know when you decide to make your arrangement with her a permanent one. We'll throw you a party."

Rob slowly sat down. "Are you giving me an ultimatum?"

"No, I'm giving you the honest truth, Peterson. If you want my support, and others' as well, you're going to need to do as we say. We don't want even a hint of impropriety being linked with us, and that will surely happen if you continue to go on as you have, squiring around a different lady friend every week."

"Is there another reason you called, sir?"

Scott didn't catch his sarcasm. "As a matter of fact, yes. I'd like you to look into the possibility of encouraging some big businesses our way."

Rob pulled out a pen and poised it above his paper. "Tell me more," he said, writing down William Scott's directives. But all the while, he was staring at the door, willing Anna to walk through and make his life the way it had been just two weeks ago.

Chapter 7

Chopping wood had never felt so beneficial, Henry thought as he once again raised the ax over his shoulder and let it fall. The blade hit the thick trunk with a reassuring *clack*, raining splinters of bark and wood to the grass below.

In no time, the tree would be felled and he could then begin the painstaking job of chopping it into firewood.

As his muscles strained, Henry welcomed the feeling. It enabled him to concentrate on the job at hand instead of the other thoughts warring in his mind and making his head spin. Jess. Rachel. Anna.

Anna.

As the ax met the wood again, Henry swallowed hard. Anna had surprised him yesterday when she'd joined him in burying Jess. She'd also surprised him by putting his needs before hers. It was now hard to imagine how he'd spent so many years only thinking of her as selfish and self-serving.

Of being merely frivolous and concerned with outward vanities instead of inner integrity. Nowadays, those thoughts shamed him. He was enough of a man to find fault with himself and wish he'd been better. He should have recognized his faults where she was concerned. He should have expected to find only the best from Anna . . . like he did of himself and the other members of his order.

After all, wasn't that how the Lord asked him to behave? "Whatsoever a man soweth, he shall also reap."

If he were honest with himself—which he found hard at times—Henry knew he would be best served by remembering that it was not just her character he was concerned about . . . but also his.

How was it possible for him to be thinking of the curly-haired beauty in any terms other than the ones that were in the most general way? They could never be a match.

Never have a future—not unless one of them was willing to change their lifestyle completely. He most certainly did not plan to do that.

From the time he was old enough to look at the world around him, Henry had known he was happy where he was. The Amish were his people, and he'd never felt alone or out of sorts, the way he'd heard other men speak of at Sunday socials. He'd hardly spent any time in the outside world during his *rumschpringe*, his running-around years. And though he enjoyed reading the city paper every once in a while and counted many English as his friends, their way of life and modern conveniences held no appeal to him. In truth, Henry felt far more interest in *The Budget*, the Amish newspaper.

He was far more at peace in his own community . . . and

in God's world. He was content to follow the traditions of his father and grandfather and the many generations who had worked the land before him. He'd looked forward to marrying Rachel and working the land near the bed and breakfast. To abiding by the principles they both had held dear.

Anna Metzger did not fit in with his past, his way of life, or his dreams for the future.

And, contrary to what she might think, he did not begrudge her for her beliefs. Everyone had the right to live how he or she saw fit. There was nothing wrong with each person following his or her given path. Anna's path was far different, that was all. She'd grown up with different expectations.

Their paths shouldn't have ever crossed for any length of time. They weren't expected to. Later, when Anna was no longer using their inn as a safe haven, she would be gone, most likely to never return.

So why did he find himself thinking of her expressive green eyes when he closed his own each evening? Why was he remembering her smile of encouragement when he sanded the piece of maple he was working on? Or her laugh when he drove his buggy to the market just the past afternoon?

Why was he reliving the feeling of hope that had filled him when she'd walked by his side, lifting his spirits, making him realize that Jess had been a good companion, but that it was his time to go . . . just as it would be his time one day as well.

More chips fell to the ground as his ax cut into the wood. Above him, the branches trembled, signaling that his work was almost done. Soon, the tree would come tumbling down, bringing with it years of growth, birds' nests, and insects' homes.

Just like he feared his life would be, if he continued to let

Anna play a part in it. Yes, the tree was about to have another purpose in the Lord's creation. One of good use . . . firewood.

But just like his life, his path, Henry knew that use wasn't what God had intended. God had intended for the tree to grow tall and strong, supporting years of growth and change. To be homes for the multitude of animals in the woods. Not to be burned for fuel in a matter of minutes.

Crack! The noise caught him unawares as the tree shook, then broke. Henry stepped back in a rush, watching the tall limbs above him come tumbling down. With a sharp rustle, branches broke and leaves crunched as they met the floor of the woods. Birds squawked and wings flapped as they flew to safety. Then, all was silence.

Henry used that time to pray for guidance . . . and to pray for Anna. He prayed for her safety.

But, to his consternation, he also prayed that she would see that her path in life was far from his. That they were not supposed to find any common ground.

And, to his complete shame and consternation, he prayed that she would leave very, very soon.

No longer did it feel strange to get up before dawn. As Anna splashed water over her face and hurriedly got dressed in the dim light from the kerosene lamp, she realized how easily she'd accepted the Brennemans' way of life in the last three weeks.

Now, first thing every morning, she accompanied Katie to the henhouse to gather eggs and then got to work making the day's bread and rolls. Little by little, as the sun rose to start their day, other Brennemans would stop in the kitchen. Mr. Brenneman came first, always taking the time to wish her good morning. Never much of a morning eater, Anna would serve John a bowl of oatmeal before he went to the barn to tend to the cows and the milking.

Next came Irene, bustling with lists and information about the night's borders. Katie would sip on a cup of coffee before going into the main dining room to quickly shine everything free of dust and set out plates, silverware, and napkins.

Anna would do her best to help Mrs. Brenneman prepare the breakfast meal. She'd gotten quite good at making scrambled eggs, if she did say so herself.

And finally, always as if he were waiting to the very last minute, Henry would appear, his tawny brown hair damp and the blanket of sleep still seeming to surround him. A mumbled *gut morning* would be followed by a complete concentration on the food she placed in front of him. Little by little, as he ingested the food and drank cup after cup of coffee, his brown eyes would brighten.

After the first few uncomfortable days, Anna had given up attempting to converse with Henry. Though he was so obviously not a morning person, she couldn't help but realize that it wasn't merely the time of day that kept things stilted between them.

No, there was more than that, and all of it was hard to even speak of. They made do by sharing glances. Though there was no animosity between them, Anna felt an awareness toward Henry different from any other Brenneman.

On some days Anna was certain she could feel his eyes on her, watching her every move. Vanity would kick in, and suddenly Anna would wish for even the smallest bit of makeup. Mascara or lipstick. Anything to brighten her eyes or face, to have him think more of her.

Which was wrong and she knew it. They had no future, and she should have been learning to care less about her vanity.

Of course, that was just one of the ways she still had trouble fitting in. She stumbled on the simplest of Pennsylvania Dutch words, still managed to offend at least one Brenneman a day with her desire to help in all the wrong ways.

To her embarrassment, she'd also spoken a time or two without thought, complaining about the scratchy dress or the pins in her hair, or her desire to just sit and watch TV.

No matter how hard she tried, it was obvious that she would never fit in. Or, she wouldn't fit in without a lot more trials and errors on her part.

That morning, after the men had been fed, Katie and Anna were in charge of placing warm Danishes and plates of eggs, homemade sausage, and bacon out for the guests.

"You take the juice out first, wouldja, Anna?" Katie asked. "I need a minute or two more to get the eggs to rights."

"All right." To her surprise, a number of people were already standing in the dining room, sipping coffee from the pot Mrs. Brenneman had placed out just moments before.

Seeing the curious eyes regarding her, Anna stumbled slightly, almost spilling the juice over her pale lavender dress and black apron.

One woman stepped to her side. "Want some help with that?" Her voice had a New York accent, and it sounded jarring to Anna's ears. She'd become so accustomed to the distinctive lilt of the Amish.

"No. *Danke*," she whispered. After righting the pitcher she carried, Anna placed it on the sideboard. Worried of being seen as an imposter, she kept her gaze down.

"Oh. No problem," the lady replied before joining the other eight or so people in the room, merrily discussing their rooms and some of the many Plain crafts they intended to buy at the flea market that they were preparing to visit.

After wiping off the side of the pitcher with a dishcloth, Anna turned toward the safety of the kitchen. Being around so many strange faces did make her feel uncomfortable. With some surprise, Anna wondered if it was because she was becoming used to the confining lifestyle of the Amish. Or was it something else?

Something didn't feel right. The same feeling had risen when she'd known it was time to hide from Rob signaled that she needed to be aware. Conscious that there was another in the room besides just tourists. Wasn't there?

"Miss, do you have any tea?"

Her heart pounded. *"Jah."* Oh, she hoped they wouldn't notice how strange and awkward she sounded! Or how nervous! Struggling to sound more nonchalant, she said slowly, "Herbal?"

"Yes, please. Thank you."

"All right." Anna had just turned when she caught another woman's eye. That lady was staring at her in surprise, tilting her head to one side as if she couldn't be sure what she was seeing.

Anna felt like doing the same thing. She knew that woman, those red curls, beautiful rosy skin, and tawny-colored eyes. Miriam Whitney. She had been a friend of her mother's since high school and had been a frequent guest at their home, especially in the summers when Mrs. Whitney and her mother played golf together.

For a moment, Anna was afraid she wasn't going to be able to breathe.

Miriam's eyes narrowed for a moment. Anna tried to look as serene and distant as possible, then hurriedly turned to make her escape.

Anna quickly pushed open the swinging door and launched into Katie. "There's someone out there I know."

Katie's eyes widened. "Really! Who?"

"The lady with short red hair. She's a friend of my mother's. She was staring at me—I think she recognized me, too. I can't go out there again."

"You think she might know your Rob?"

"I don't think she does, but I can't risk her telling my mother. By now my mom has probably figured out I never went to Florida and is wondering where I am."

"And then your mother could tell Rob and he'd find you."

Feeling tears of stress fill her eyes, Anna proclaimed, "I'm so sorry. I'm a mess right now. For a while I thought I was safe."

"You are safe," Katie said soothingly. "Don't worry so much. You mustn't borrow trouble."

"I can't help but worry. I know I can't hide forever." Hands shaking, Anna pressed them against her thighs. "For the last couple of days, I'd almost thought I could."

"Don't fret so, Anna. Sit down for a moment."

"A lady wants tea." Anna closed her eyes, hearing the desperation evident in her voice. "Herbal tea."

Katie patted her shoulder comfortingly. "That's no problem. We fix herbal teas all the time."

"If I prepare it, will you bring it out?"

"Of course I will, Anna."

Henry came in just as the tea was steeping. "Taking a rest already, Anna? When will you ever do your fair share?"

Anna almost lashed out at him until she heard the teasing note in his voice, saw the amusement in his eyes. Finally, Henry Brenneman felt comfortable enough around her to joke. And tease.

This final acceptance of her felt like a hug . . . and made her want to burst into tears. She had become attached—had started to feel real friendship toward him.

When he gazed at her a moment longer, Anna knew he was waiting for a reply. "You know me, always lazy," she said brightly, though her voice cracked and effectively ruined the pert comment.

True concern washed over his features. "What's wrong? What happened to you?"

"Hush now, Henry," Katie chided. "Anna knows someone out there. In the dining room." Brushing past her brother importantly, Katie picked up the tray of tea, the carafe, and a small towel. "Move to the side, please. I've tea to deliver."

In a flash, the swinging doors opened and shut as Katie's bright blue skirts disappeared from view.

Anna's heart slammed in her chest as she heard the guests speak to Katie.

Henry took the chair by her side. "Who do you know?"

"Miriam Whitney. Mrs. Whitney's an old friend of my mother's. I've known her since I was in grade school."

"You sure she's who you saw?"

"I'm positive. She's a nice lady, but I know she recognized me. What am I going to do?"

Henry winked at her. "Breathe, Anna. Even if someone

thinks she knows you, she'll never assume you've turned Plain. You had made a wise decision when you chose to hide here. No one would suspect you to be here, dressed like us and servin' tea."

Put that way, Anna supposed Henry was right. She knew of very few people in her former life who even thought about the Amish more than characters in a movie or quaint people in a postcard. They'd certainly never consider joining their ranks.

"That's better," he said soothingly, even going so far as to pat her shoulder.

She'd just taken his advice and breathed deep when she heard the low echo of Miriam's voice. "Where's the other girl? She seemed so familiar."

Anna couldn't hear Katie's reply because everything seemed to be roaring in her own ears.

Both she and Henry stared at the doorway when Katie appeared again, her face white.

"What happened?"

"That lady asked about you." With a stricken expression, Katie added, "Lord, please forgive me, but I lied! I . . . I told her you were my cousin!"

Henry blinked. "Katie, you shouldn't have told her anything!"

"I tried not to, but she kept staring at me. And, what is worse, I don't think she believed me, Anna."

"It's okay. There's nothing to be done," Anna said, though inside, her heart was breaking. She was going to have to leave—if Miriam happened to say anything to her mother, and there was a very good chance that would happen, her mother could tell Rob. Next thing they knew, he would appear, endangering her and all the Brennemans.

And what would she do then? Leave with Rob? Anna shuddered to think of what her life would be like then.

"I need to go tend to them again," Katie said awkwardly, her arms now loaded with a plate of apple muffins. "They're waitin' for their breakfast, for sure."

To Anna's great surprise, Henry picked up the platter of sausage and eggs. "I'll help, Katie. You go to the barn," he whispered. "Go to my tack room and wait."

"Are you sure?"

"I am. Go now, Anna."

Anna threw on a cloak and hurried to the barn. The brisk air whipped against her face, but while she'd found it invigorating before dawn, she only felt the sharp sting of the wind now. After slipping in through the side door, she headed straight to Henry's workshop. In seconds, she opened and shut the door, firmly closing out even more of the outside world.

Her hands and legs were shaking so much that she sat down on his stool before they gave out underneath her.

Little by little, her breathing slowed, and once again she was able to think reasonably. It was time to think of other people, time to put them before herself, no matter what the cost was to her.

As she recognized Henry's comforting scent in the room, Katie knew she had no choice; she was going to have to leave. She'd been a fool to think that she fit in, that she could hide at the Brennemans'.

Once more, she was ashamed to realize that Henry's dire prediction had come true . . . she had, once again, put her own needs first and in so doing, had endangered all the Brennemans. She'd done exactly what she'd naively promised she would never do. . . . she put the very people who had offered her solace in the grip of danger.

In four hours, after the first round of visitors had checked out and left, Anna would follow.

She had no choice.

"Lord, please help me," she whispered. "I now know that I should have completely repented for my sins weeks ago. I repent now and am truly sorry.

"Glorious God, please help me find the strength to stand on my own two feet and come to grips with all the doubts that fill me. Give me strength to accept my faults and to not run. It's time to begin again."

Closing her eyes, Anna continued to pray with all her might. She just hoped God would see fit to help and guide her—and not see her repentance as too little, too late.

Meredith's hands shook as she set the receiver back on the phone.

"Who was that?"

"Calvin, that was Miriam Whitney."

He coughed, making Meredith recall that he never really had enjoyed Miriam's company. "What did she want? To tell you that latest gossip on her street?"

"Calvin, she's not that bad."

"I certainly think she is! Why, if that woman paid half as much attention to herself as everyone around her, she'd have a whole lot less health problems. She has more ailments than anyone I've ever met. And if she's not complaining about her joints or her hip, she's spreading rumors about everyone she knows."

Meredith closed her eyes and tried to keep her patience. "She wasn't calling to gossip."

"What did she want?"

"To tell me that she thinks she saw Anna."

Calvin froze. Slowly stepping forward, he searched her face. "What? Where?"

"In Amish country."

He rolled his eyes. "Who else did she see? George Bush?"

For a moment, Meredith smiled before shaking her head. "Actually, Miriam said she saw Anna at the Brenneman Bed and Breakfast."

"That place sounds familiar."

Meredith noticed he wasn't laughing now. "It is familiar. Years ago, Anna and I spent a weekend there, learning to quilt. From what I recall, she and one of the daughters have kept in touch."

"Is that allowed? I didn't think the Amish were encouraged to keep relationships with outsiders."

Meredith shrugged. "No, many Amish have English friends. What's rarer, I think, is for two teenage girls from such different backgrounds to keep in touch for so many years—especially through letters! It seems most teenagers only pay attention to who they see a lot. I recall Anna mentioning that she would pay a visit to the Brennemans once a year or so. She sent them Christmas cards, too . . . and that the daughter always teased her about them."

"Would Anna go to them?"

"I don't know. Miriam said that Anna looked Amish . . .

she was dressed Plainly, in their clothes . . . but she recognized Anna because of her distinctive green eyes."

"Nothing to think about, dear. Let's get dressed and go get her."

She laid a hand on his arm. "I'm not sure if that's wise. I've gotten the feeling that we haven't seen the last of Rob. What if he's following us?"

"That sounds a bit paranoid, Meredith. I doubt even he would do something like that."

"A month ago, I would have agreed, but now I'm not so sure. Every time we've been in contact with him, Rob has acted strange and angry. Now I don't believe I'd put anything past him." After a moment's hesitation, she admitted the rest of her worries. "I'm afraid of how he'd retaliate if we even tried to stand in his way."

Calvin slowly sat down. "So what are we going to do? Call the police?"

"Calvin, I think we should wait a bit. If that really was Anna at the Brennemans', then she's safe. The Brennemans are good people, and I know that they will be vigilant about caring for her."

"Even though I'd rather our daughter be back here at home, I'm sure you're right." Her husband of forty years stood up and walked to the fireplace. As was his habit, he brushed a hand lovingly over the mahogany mantel they'd bought in auction years ago.

But where once the gesture brought a pleased smile from him, now it was obvious that all of their material possessions paled in comparison to what was really at stake . . . their only daughter. "What are we going to say to Miriam? What did you tell her?"

"I didn't say much of anything. I laughed off Miriam's hunch and said that Anna was in Florida."

"Do you think she believed you?"

"I'm sure she did. I mean, why wouldn't she? The only thing worse than not having anything to gossip about would be to get caught gossiping with the wrong information. We aren't alone," she said softly. "Anna is in God's hands. He guided her to safety, and I truly feel He's placed His loving arms around her. Maybe we should ask Him for His help, too."

"For us?"

"Definitely. I need His blessings and guidance more than ever."

Calvin murmured, "Do we deserve it?"

"No," she said with a smile. "We don't deserve His guidance at all . . . but that's the beauty of grace, is it not?"

He walked to her and took her hand. "Oh, Meredith. What would I do without you? You make everything better."

"I wish that were true." As far as she was concerned, she'd failed her daughter. She was ashamed. If that girl was indeed her daughter, Anna had taken refuge with another woman's family. And that for whatever reason, they'd seen the need to protect her far more quickly than she had.

Chapter 8

Henry wished Anna Metzger had never come into his life. If she hadn't, he wouldn't be feeling the things he did right at that moment—panic, longing, and resignation.

He was captivated. He longed to hold her in his arms.

He knew why—it was no great mystery. He was pining for her, thinking about a future with Anna. Wondering if there was anything he could've done better in order to comfort her, to give her hope and solace.

And all of it without his family finding out.

These discordant feelings were unfamiliar and troublesome. Intrigue and secrets were not part of his life, nor were they for anyone he knew. It was the Amish way to speak without rancor, to speak from the heart. With sincerity and frankness. People did not keep secrets. They did not covet things they could not have.

They did not lie, not even to themselves.

Henry slowed his pace as he wondered just how long he could continue to deceive himself about his attraction to Anna. Not much longer, he knew that to be true. There was something about her green eyes that drew him to her. Made his gaze last a little too long whenever she was nearby. Made him dream of things that could never happen. Made him want to protect her, when just days ago, he'd only wanted to protect himself.

Squaring his shoulders, Henry quietly opened the barn door, then walked into his workshop to where Anna was. He cautioned himself to think only of her safety, not his own feelings. Not how seeing her perched on his stool made his heart glad.

She looked up when he closed the door behind him. "Hi."

He tried to smile, but it was hard to find the energy. Anna's cheeks were streaked with tears, and the sight of her sadness struck him like a blow. "Anna, are you okay?"

Wiping a cheek with a fist, she shook her head. "No."

He stepped closer, finally stopping across from her, resting the back of his thighs against the top of his workshop table. Now mere inches separated the two of them. "That lady, she moved on about a half hour ago."

"I thought I heard a couple of cars drive off. Did she ask a lot more questions?"

"Questions? Oh, *jah*." He tried to pretend to misunderstand her. "She asked about milking cows and my schooling. The usual questions."

A hint of a smile fought its way forward. "And you answered?"

"I did answer. I even told her about my carpentry business," he added, seeing how his chatter was freeing some of the gloom from her expression.

"I'm surprised."

"You shouldn't be." He jabbed his chest with two fingers. "Sometimes even I have patience."

Anna finally did smile then, her face lighting up with a beam of gratitude. "Who would've thought?"

"Not I, and that's a fact."

They shared a smile, bringing a warmth to the room that had nothing to do with heat and everything to do with their proximity. Once again, Henry knew what he was feeling was wrong. He tried to focus on the scent of wood chips and oil. On the faint movements of the horses on the other side of the wall.

On anything other than the way that one stubborn curl had sprung out of her *kapp* and framed her cheek, reminding him of just how much he'd been taken with her golden hair.

Anna stood up and put a full foot between them. "Well. Thanks for coming out here. Please tell Katie that I'll be right in to help her with the dishes and rooms."

"No hurry. I came to let you know the woman left, not to summon you to work just yet."

"Is that the only reason you came out here? To deliver a message?"

Her directness with him was new. Usually Anna sidestepped information, talked in half-truths and in vagueness. Usually that bothered him . . . he would far rather she say what was on her mind. But now that the tables were turned and he was the one fending off uncomfortable questions, he wished they could go back to their old ways. Anything to prevent him from saying too much.

"Cat got your tongue, Henry?"

"Maybe I was worried about you," he murmured. "Maybe I thought you'd be in here crying."

"You don't need to be," she replied, though her eyes still glistened with unshed tears.

"I'm afraid I do. You need someone looking out for ya."

"I need to look out for myself a little better, I'm afraid." Before he could think of a fitting response, she went on. "Henry, you were perfectly right in your assessment of me the afternoon I arrived."

He recalled the conversation and regretted his harsh words. "No, I wasn't right at all. I should have held my tongue. I treated a guest in our home shamefully, and that is a fact."

She chuckled softly. "No, I think you treated me exactly how I needed to be treated. I needed to hear your words of truth."

"Not the way I said them."

"The way you said them was fine." After a pause, she continued. "I have been putting myself first and, consequently, you all in danger."

"I don't know about danger."

A firm resolve entered her eyes. "I'm afraid I do. If Miriam talks, and she will, I'm sure of it, word will get around that I'm here. It's time I left."

The statement came so suddenly that Henry wasn't sure he heard her correctly. "Leave?"

"Yep. I'll help Katie and then pack up my things. I should be out of your lives within a few hours."

No longer did his anger and bitterness about Rachel cloud over his feelings. Instead, all things Anna came to mind. He remembered her embrace when he'd grieved for Jess, remembered her quiet company and was grateful for it. There was no way he could live with himself if he encouraged her to leave directly and make her way alone. "I hardly think that's a wise idea, Anna."

"Luckily for you, you won't need to worry about it. This time, all the responsibility for my ideas, good or bad, will rest on me."

Panic engulfed him as he envisioned Anna leaving. Just like Rachel, she'd be walking toward a way of life in which he didn't fit in and never would be able. He would stay where he was, waiting and wishing for circumstances to be different. "You're running scared. Take some time to think this through. Where would you go?"

"I don't know." She pushed back a stray curl again. Henry watched it return to rest upon her cheek as she spoke again. "I have some money. I did remember to take quite a bit of cash. Perhaps I'll travel to Florida, after all."

Henry knew that if she left for Florida, he'd never see her again. And though that might be the best thing for him—out of sight and mind—he knew he wasn't ready to say good-bye to her yet. "You can't keep running," he said slowly, like he was just realizing the consequences her actions would have. "Sooner or later you'll have to stop."

"I know that, but I also know I can't stay here. Rob will find me, if he wants to. And I'm afraid he's going to want to find me very badly. As far as he's concerned, I'm *his*. I also know things about his financial dealings that could ruin him."

"Then tell the authorities."

"They might not believe me. Rob is a well-respected lawyer, running for office with a great many influential people backing him up. I don't know for certain, but I'm very afraid that he's got quite a few other elected officials—including his brother-in-law who's a sheriff—on his payroll. Even if they don't approve of Rob's ways, I know they're not going to risk losing their own livelihoods."

"Perhaps you could make them see the benefits of helping you. Seems to me more often than not, people do care about what is right and good."

"I hope that's true." A bright, sudden smile transformed her features until worry replaced her expression once again. "It won't be easy. I wouldn't even know where to begin."

Unfortunately, he didn't know exactly how to aid her, either. He knew few English. And though he did know a few men who left their order, Henry hadn't kept in close enough contact with them to help Anna in any appreciable way.

But that didn't stop his need for her. Desperate, Henry tried again. "Wait a day or so, then. At least do that, wouldja?"

"Why?"

Awareness sparked between them, making Henry recognize that Anna wasn't as oblivious to their connection as he'd tried to pretend she was.

Amazing how, now that he'd come to know her, Henry realized she was far different and more thoughtful than he'd ever imagined.

Before, he'd turned Anna into a lazy, silly, fancy girl. Now, he knew her to be looking for acceptance and comfort, just like he was. For a split second, he considered asking her to stay with them forever. To adopt their ways and join their order. Then, with God's help, one day he'd have the right and opportunity to pledge himself to her.

But that was as impossible to imagine as wishing Jess to rise up from his grave. Some things were over and done with, and it would be best if they all came to grips with that.

He didn't want to say good-bye. Not yet. But it wasn't his way to voice his innermost thoughts . . . and it wasn't Anna's way to merely listen and not act.

Because of all these things, he stayed silent.

Inadvertently, his silence seemed to answer her question.

Hurt and a sad kind of resolve filled her gaze. "I see."

"You don't." He opened his mouth, to try to verbalize his feelings, but old hurts and thoughts of what could never be got in the way. To push her so wasn't his way, and wasn't the best thing for her.

Thirty seconds flowed into one minute, then two.

Moving toward the door, she shook her head in dismay. "Thanks for letting me hide in here, Henry, but I think we both know it's time I left. I can't hide in your workshop or at the Brenneman Bed and Breakfast any longer."

"But—"

She held up a hand. "But most of all, I can't hide from myself."

It happened before he was aware of it. He reached out and took her hand. Linked his fingers with hers. Stunned, she stilled, her lips parted.

Did she feel the same connection that he did? "Don't," he whispered. "Don't go away. Yet."

Her hand still folded into his, Henry was aware of her soft, smooth skin. The way her fingers linked around his, curved, so delicate and sweet in his own work-roughened hands.

He didn't want to let her go.

The surge of awareness he felt for her was nothing he'd anticipated, asked for, or could control. "I don't know what's happening," he said honestly. "I can only tell you that it's taken me by surprise."

Still looking at their linked fingers, Anna carefully caressed his knuckles with her thumb, the nail cut short and looking pink and perfect. "Do you want me to say it?" She swallowed. Shrugged her shoulders. "All right. After all, I guess I have nothing to lose, do I?"

He shook his head to stop her, but she'd already continued. "I . . . I am starting to have feelings for you. Feelings that are more than mere friendship. I'm sorry."

Inside, his pulse leaped. Inside, his heart pounded with the knowledge that Rachel hadn't taken everything from him. No, instead of stealing his heart, she'd only injured it, and before he knew it, his heart was beating again, strong and true. Showing him that life could go on. And maybe—just maybe—he and Rachel had never been meant to be, if already he was tempted by another. "We're different, you and I."

"I know," she said quickly. "Please don't ask me to apologize. I just don't think I can tell you that I'm sor—"

He cut her off. "I wasn't going to do that. Anna, I was going to say that I, too, feel that way."

Eyes widening, she pulled her hand away from his. "You do?"

"I do." He felt the loss of their connection just as strongly as if someone had removed his shirt. Suddenly, he felt cool and vulnerable. Open to her prying eyes.

As Anna continued to stare, her gaze full of wonder and

the faint feel of hope, Henry hung his head, feeling like a giant load had been lifted from his shoulders, only to land on his foot.

Once again, Anna took the first step forward. "You look upset."

"I am upset. I don't know what to do. I don't know what to do about you and me."

"Perhaps we could just remain friends."

"Have we become friends?" Yes, he did feel more comfortable around her, and he'd valued her companionship when he'd buried Jess, but he didn't feel friendship for her. No, it was more like a very strong awareness, shaking him in his soul.

"I hope so. All I do know is that I could sure use a friend right now."

"Then I will be a friend for you. Only a friend. Just don't leave."

"I'll speak to your parents. I need to tell them just what might happen if Rob discovers where I am."

"Their minds won't change. They'll continue to offer shelter."

"I'll be grateful, but also feel guilty if something were to happen. Henry, I just don't know if I can shoulder that burden now, as well."

He stepped forward. Took a risk and wiped the last tear track on her translucent cheek. The skin there was as soft and feathery sweet as he'd ever imagined. "I'll walk you inside, then."

"Because we're friends?"

"Because unless our worlds change, that's all we can ever be."

Chapter 9

She did wait. One week.

"And so, you see, Mr. and Mrs. Brenneman, there is a very good reason for me to be going," Anna finished, feeling fairly proud of herself because her voice didn't come out as shaky as she felt. "I think it would be best if I left you in peace."

Mr. Brenneman leaned forward, bracing his elbows on his knees. The five of them were seated in the hearth room. "I think it's too late for the peace you're speaking of, Anna."

Irene nodded. "Your presence has disrupted our household mightily."

Katie looked as if she were about to cry. *"Mamm."*

"Hush, daughter," Mr. Brenneman commanded. "Anna has disrupted our home, there is no doubt of that."

Anna felt as if she couldn't breathe. Their stern expressions were repressive, their words as stinging to her person as an ice storm. "It won't take me long to pack my bags."

"We didn't ask you to leave, though," Mr. Brenneman said.

They'd done everything but say those words. Standing up, Anna murmured, "It's not necessary. I'll be out of here soon."

Katie stood up, too. "Anna's my *gut* friend. She's done more than her share of work. *Mamm*, you saw how the guests were mightily pleased with her cloverleaf rolls. And she's ironed—"

"Hush, daughter," her father said again. Turning to Anna, he said, "I think perhaps it's time for you to speak to your parents."

"I would agree, except I don't know if I can trust them."

Irene's gaze softened. "You'd doubt your mother's love?"

"I know she loves me, but I doubt that she completely understands just how bad things are with Rob."

"Give her another chance. Imagine what Jesus would have done if He would have settled for doubt and distrust. Sometimes a message needs to be delivered more than once."

The thought of calling her parents, of asking for their help just to be denied again, was scarier than the thought of surviving on her own. "I can't."

This time it was Henry who stood up. "Give them a chance, Anna. Now you have us. Now you know we can help you. Give them a chance."

As if the whole conversation was settled, Mr. Brenneman walked to the doorway. "I'll go get your phone out of hiding and you can call your parents. I'm sure they're worried about you by now."

When he left the room, Mrs. Brenneman patted her on the shoulder, then exited as well, leaving Anna with only Henry and Katie for company.

Katie's lovely blue eyes were bright with unshed tears. "I'm so sorry, Anna. I thought my parents would surely listen better."

"They have listened," Henry corrected. "And I have to say I agree with their words. We canna move forward until we come to terms with our past."

John Brenneman entered the room and with little fanfare, handed Anna the phone. "Would you like our company while you call or would you rather be alone?"

Anna was afraid if she was left by herself, she'd be afraid to punch in the numbers. "I need all of you here," she said.

"Call then, dear Anna. No use waiting any more."

Four interested faces watched her push the power button on her phone. "I'm waiting for a signal," she said when they all looked at her like it was about to start ringing. When the bands of a good signal came into view, Anna gathered her courage and dialed her parents.

The phone rang once. Twice. Finally, after the fourth ring, the message center clicked on. Though she was afraid to leave a message, especially since Rob could be monitoring her messages, Anna took a leap of faith and spoke. If she didn't step forward into the open, she might never be free to move forward. "Mom, Dad, it's me. Anna. I, um, never went to Miami. I've been hiding from Rob. I'm at the Brennemans'. You know, the Amish B and B we used to go to for the quilting classes. Come out for me, would you? I need you. I love you, too. "

She clicked off. "They weren't home," she said unnecessarily, and feeling more than a little let down. But what had she expected? That her parents would be sitting by their phone, just waiting for her to contact them?

Those days were long gone—if they'd ever been there at all.

Henry, to Anna's surprise, leaped to the rescue. "When they get home and listen to messages, they'll be pleased to hear from you, mark my words. Before you know it, we'll be looking out the window and watching your parents come walking in."

To her surprise, Anna realized she, too, was hoping for that day. "I hope it's soon." Now that the call had been made and with the conversation with Henry so fresh in her mind, Anna was ready to reach some resolutions.

"I'd be mighty surprised if it wasn't soon." With a smile, Katie added, "Then we'll see if they recognize you, dressed all Plain like you are."

"They might. No one has your eyes, Anna Metzger."

There it was, once again. A sudden pull toward Henry that was filled with unspoken words and quiet promises. Quickly, she peeked at Katie to see her reaction.

As usual, Katie said nothing—merely looked at Henry thoughtfully, her gaze knowing and silent.

But at the moment, there were too many other obstacles in the way to think of relationships.

Anna clicked off the power on her phone. "Thanks for encouraging me to do this. I am glad I reached out to them."

"I am, as well."

"If you don't mind, I'll just go put the phone back in my suitcase. I trust myself a lot more now than I used to."

"That's a *gut* idea, dear Anna," Mrs. Brenneman said. "And then you must help me in the kitchen."

Katie rushed out to do a chore, leaving the room empty

except for she and Henry. "Thank you," she said. "I needed to do this."

"I know you did."

"About earlier—"

"Let's not speak of it. I don't want to forget our words, but perhaps we should remember that things need to happen in their own time."

"Having time sounds mighty wondrous."

Henry laughed. "Anna Metzger, just that moment, you sounded Amish. Almost like one of us."

As Anna went back to her room, her steps faltered. This afternoon, she'd been more aware than ever before that she wasn't one of them . . . and to everyone concerned, she would never be.

Chapter 10

Meredith played the message one more time. After a loud *beep*, Anna's voice filtered through the small speaker on the phone. Her pulse raced. *"Mom, Dad, it's me. Anna."*

Turning toward Calvin, she raised an eyebrow. "Well? What do you think after hearing it for a third time?"

"Just about the same thing I did when I heard the message the first. Anna sounds good. Like herself."

Meredith bit her lip they continued to listen to Anna's too-short message. *"I'm at the Brennemans'. You know, the Amish B and B. . ."*

"Do you think so?" she asked. "Do you think Anna sounds nervous? Worried?"

"If she does, I don't know what we could do about it."

"Calvin!"

"Mer, Anna probably is worried. She's probably worried

about what we're going to say when we finally see her." He tapped the machine. "I, for one, would like to wring our daughter's neck. I think I've aged ten years since she took off."

"I don't imagine Anna is sitting around worried about getting in trouble. I think she knows she is still in trouble." She paused. "Maybe things are even worse, and that's why she finally called us."

Calvin walked around the kitchen island and reached for her. "Don't worry, Mer," he said. "After all, she's where she wants to be, where she feels safe."

Meredith heard the bitterness in her husband's voice and knew it came from hurt. No matter what he said, Calvin was disappointed Anna hadn't tried harder to seek their help. "I suppose." She stepped into his arms and finally let herself let go. After over a month of worry, they now knew Anna was okay. Within hours, they'd be with her, patching things up. Developing a plan of how to break her free from Rob's clutches. Everything would be back to normal. How it used to be. With a sigh, her shoulders relaxed.

The horrible, terrible ordeal was almost over.

Cal gently smoothed her hair from her brow and pressed his lips to her forehead. "You know, it's going to break my heart not to go see her."

His statement practically sent Meredith to her knees. "What are you talking about?" she asked, jerking away from him. "She called us. *Finally* called us! We have no choice but to go to the Brennemans and pick her up."

"We can't do that. Rob's been driving by here on a regular basis. I've seen other strange cars parked out in front of the house for hours at night. If we suddenly took a trip out to

Amish country, there's a very good chance he or someone who works for him might be suspicious."

She waved a hand in dismissal. "You're getting ahead of yourself. There's no way Rob is watching us that closely, and even if he was, he wouldn't know where we were headed. I doubt he's going to care. Besides, what does it matter? Once we have Anna, everything will be fine." Her voice cracked but she covered it up with a smile. Someone had to believe everything was going to be okay.

"I doubt it."

Her husband's sarcastic tone caught her off guard. Had Calvin really become so hard over the last month? "You need to have faith, darling. With God's help, everything is going to work out just fine."

He shook his head in irritation—and shook off her hand on his shoulder. "You, Meredith, need to stop being so naive. Rob is watching us. And I don't think anything is going to stop him from trying to get Anna. This isn't just a case of a man missing his girl. She knows something, or else she has something that he wants."

"I know . . . but—"

"We know enough. We just can't risk it, Mer. We can't."

Nothing he said held any meaning for her. She had to go to Anna. "We're not prisoners, and we shouldn't act as if we are. Even if you won't go, I'm going to get in the car."

"No."

"She asked for us." Meredith bit her tongue, holding back the obvious. Finally. She'd finally asked for her parents.

"It's time we faced the facts. Anna must know something about Rob. This stalking nonsense can't just be about some re-lationship that's gone south. She must know something about his work or his personal life or his campaign." He drummed his fingers on the counter. "There's got to be some information he didn't want made public that she must have discovered. Something really powerful—powerful enough to compromise his bid for the election. She's in danger."

Her mouth went dry. Steadying herself, Meredith said, "If she's in danger, then that's all the more reason that we need to go to her." Memories of a much different time sprang forth. Meredith remembered a time when Anna was in middle school. One afternoon she'd come home with a broken heart, straight into her mother's arms. It had taken hours of long conversation in order to make her happy, to dry her tears. "I can't ignore her, Calvin. I can't let her just sit there, all alone."

"She's not. She's with the Brennemans. They're looking after her."

"It's not the same as her parents."

"No, it's not. We didn't believe her when she told us about Rob, did we?" Bitterness tinged his next words as he continued. "We ignored everything she said and were going to force her to continue to see Peterson."

"You're not being fair. I'm not going to let you win this one."

"It's not a win-lose game here, Meredith."

"I'm not playing a game." Panic rose in her throat as she totally grasped everything Calvin was saying. "We can't ignore her. Anna is going to be looking for us. She's going to be expecting us."

"We can't go there. Not until we know for sure that Rob isn't following our every move."

"But Cal—"

"Right now she's safe." Almost in a whisper he added, "What if *we* put her in danger? What if we unknowingly led Rob to her? *Then* what would we do?"

She wouldn't be able to go on. That's what would happen.

Thoroughly defeated, Meredith stared at the speaker phone. "What are you suggesting?"

Calvin erased Anna's recording. "Let's begin to think offensively. There must be someone we know who will either work around Rob Peterson or not be intimidated by the man."

The recorder beeped, letting them know the erasure was successful. Hearing that made it feel as if they were losing Anna all over again. "Anything else?" she asked.

"Well . . . is there anyone we could trust to go to the Brennemans' for us and relay a message? Anyone who Rob wouldn't be suspicious of and follow?"

That was a good idea. It was just too bad that everyone she was thinking of couldn't be completely trusted to either keep her silence or not get involved. Or, they were in such poor health that Meredith was reluctant to involve them in something so potentially dangerous. "I can't think of anyone off the top of my head."

He reached out for her again, asking without words to trust him. To have faith. "I just had an idea."

"Who?"

"Beverly Lowrey."

"Beverly? She must be almost seventy years old!"

For the first time during their conversation, Calvin grinned. "We both know Beverly would have your head if she heard you describe her as too old for anything."

"She's too old for this. We can't put her in danger."

"But what if she makes that choice on her own? She's one

of the gutsiest people I know. She's also one of the most reliable people."

"But do you think she'd want to get involved?"

Calvin squeezed her hand, gifting her with the first genuine smile in a long time. "I think she'd love to get involved. I think she'd jump at the chance to do a little something other than crosswords and make her weekly trip to the grocery store."

"You may be right. If Beverly wants to help, I can't think of anyone better," she said.

But that was a lie. More than anything, Meredith wanted to be the one to make everything better.

And once again, she wasn't even going to come close.

Tracy Cleese was perky, brunette, and had the type of figure that was hard for a man to ignore. Rob hadn't even tried.

Not that Tracy had been around all that long. After William Scott had delivered his ultimatum, Rob had gotten busy and started making calls to anyone who might know of a woman who was suitable for him to be seen with publicly.

Tracy had been the strongest contender. A recent graduate of Ohio State, she'd been in a number of going-nowhere jobs and living at home. He'd met her at a coffee shop for a first date, then taken her to a trendy spot for lunch the following day. Both times, she'd been pleasant, easily distracted, and had looked fabulous.

She definitely had possibilities, if one overlooked the fact that she was almost too easy to bend to his will and had no conversational skills beyond her hair, her diet, or her miniature poodle, Fluff.

"Rob, are you sure you want me to work here with you?"

She giggled before continuing coyly, "I'm just not sure if we want that kind of relationship."

"I'm sure."

"Okay. But if I do something you don't like, let me know, would you?"

"I promise I will," he said, though Rob's mind was on Tracy's looks and not her words. Her smile was suggestive. Too suggestive and obvious.

The conservative constituents in the county would take one look at that and make a beeline for the door. No one wanted their congressman hooked up with a floozy.

Mentally, Rob made a note to bring in another girl, soon.

Figuring everything between them was peachy, Tracy blathered on about the sale at Nordstrom's before working quietly on some files when the phone rang. "Rob Peterson's office. Tracy speaking. Oh, yeah. Sure." Brown eyes batted as she pushed down Hold. "It's for you, Rob."

As if it was going to be for anyone else. "Peterson."

"Rob, it's Grant."

His worthless brother-in-law. "Do you have any information for me?"

"Not yet."

"Another week's gone by. What have you been doing?"

His brother-in-law's voice turned hard. "I've been working. There are actual cases that need to be taken care of, you know."

"Actual? What is that supposed to mean?"

"Anna isn't even classified as a missing person yet. The Metzgers haven't even contacted their local police. Rob, I bet Anna is sitting on the beach somewhere. I bet she's going to

be laughing her head off when she finds out you've been looking all over for her. She's going to make a fool out of you."

A fool? Every cell in Rob's body wanted to reach through
the phone and punch his worthless relative and tell him what
exactly he could do with his so-called job. He owed every bit
of his power and authority to Rob, and it would serve him
well to remember that. And Rob also knew Anna was nearby,
in Amish country. He could feel it. "Watch it, Grant."

"You watch it, Peterson. I warned you finding a gal in
Amish country was going to be hard . . . especially if she
doesn't want to be found."

Rob refused to give up. He was not a quitter, and never
had been. Not since his dad had told him just what happened to losers and quitters. "There's got to be some sign of
her somewhere. A girl like that wouldn't be missed easily."
Thinking of the way her green eyes were so expressive and
how more often than not, her laughter would carry far and
cause too much attention, Rob added, "I'm sure she's caused
notice somewhere."

"Maybe, maybe not. People don't always look beyond the
clothes. And if she's in disguise, we may never know what
happened to her."

Never? Panic flowed through Rob. With force, he tamped
the unwelcome emotion down. Anna was not going to disap-
pear from his life. Even if she was dead in a ditch, he had to
find her. He had to know.

Otherwise she could ruin him.

"What you are saying is unacceptable. You need to get a
deputy or someone else on this case. Full time."

"Maybe you should contact the local police."

All they would do was delve into things that were none of their business. "Not yet."

"Have you pressed her parents for more information? Maybe they know more than they're lettin' on."

"I've pressed." Anger coursed through him as he imagined what people would say if he actually had to admit he'd chased her away. If she could prove that he'd hit her multiple times.

He drummed his fingers on the desk. Would she have had the foresight to take pictures of her bruises? Had she been that devious?

Of course, even those photographs would be nothing compared to what could happen if she ever leaked exactly what he'd been doing with much of the campaign and charity contributions. If the press got hold of that, with their liberal viewpoints and propensity for stretching the truth, he'd have a full-blown storm disrupting his life. "Just keep trying."

"I already am," Grant said quietly. "You may have put me in this job, Rob, but I take it seriously. Very seriously."

Rob hung up the phone, feeling even more furious than from their earlier meeting. Where was Anna? And why would she be in Amish country?

The cloying scent of roses and honeysuckle permeated his office, followed by the baby-doll sweet voice of Tracy. "How about a cup of coffee, Rob?"

"No coffee."

"You sure? I just made a fresh pot." She patted his shoulder. "I bet it will perk you up." A giggle followed—obviously Tracy was a fan of puns.

"No."

"No? Just 'no'?" A hand popped on her hip. "Well, that's rude. The least you could do is add a 'thank you.' I'm doing all this for you, you know. A smile every now and then would be appreciated."

Tracy, with her too-long nails, too-strong perfume, and too-dumb way of speaking, was driving him to the edge. Gripping the table in order not to dissolve that cloying smile, he said, "I think it would be best for you to leave."

Down went the cup of coffee, most likely leaving a ring on his cherry desk in the process. "Leave? What are you saying? You want me to, like, quit?"

"Exactly."

"Now?"

"Immediately." Quicker if possible.

Ten minutes later, Rob found himself alone in his office, ignoring stacks of paperwork and multiple messages waiting to be returned. All he wanted to do was stare out the window and wish for things that never were.

A loser. He was becoming a loser.

That would never do.

"I'm sure there's a good reason your parents haven't stopped by," Katie said reasonably. "Perhaps they didn't receive the message? Maybe that answering machine you told me about didn't click on like it was supposed to."

Anna tried to match her friend's optimistic tone but it was hard. "That's a possibility, but I kind of doubt it."

"Or they haven't listened to the messages?"

"I couldn't imagine my parents not checking messages the minute they got home." Hanging her head, hating her self-doubts, Anna murmured, "They must not care. You heard my message. My mother knows exactly where I am. I asked her to come here, to come and get me. She doesn't want to come." Once again, they'd let her down.

"I'm sure that isn't the case. Perhaps she's on her way, Anna." Pointing to the long, winding road leading up to the inn, Katie smiled. "I betcha any minute now we'll be seeing your parents driving along in their automobile."

Unfortunately, only silence greeted them from the frost-covered streets and lanes.

"Maybe." They stared out at the road, at the back parking lot for another few moments, then unable to take it anymore, Anna turned away. It was hard to accept that her parents weren't running to her side. Hard to accept their betrayal. She felt empty inside.

Yet she knew she couldn't pass off all the blame. She, too, had acted selfishly. She hadn't tried harder to get them to believe her, merely had run and asked the Brennemans to take her in, no matter what the consequences might be. No small wonder Henry hadn't thought much of her.

Now that the fog of Rob's abuse had lifted from her shoulders, Anna saw more clearly than ever before the danger she'd put the Brennemans in.

The danger Rob was to her, and to everyone around her. Back when she was under his influence, she'd still succumbed to his flashes of kindness. She'd still sometimes been fooled by his movie-star smile and his campaign promises. Now she realized that there was nothing about Rob Peterson under that shiny facade. No, like the proverbial onion, he had no core.

At least, he didn't have one that she ever wanted to witness ever again. "What do you think I should do now?" she murmured, knowing that there was no good answer and not expecting one.

Katie shook out her skirts as she stood up, her whole being projecting a sense of purpose. "I think you should come help me clean guest rooms. *Mamm* said she expects two couples this evening, one a repeat customer."

Anna noticed for the first time that Katie, too, was gazing off into the distance, but not fixating on the paved road. No, she seemed to be looking over the hills. "Does Jonathan live out that way?"

Katie started. "Yes."

"Do you think anything's ever going to happen between you two?" Anna meant to be teasing. Comforting.

But as usual, Katie took her question very seriously. "I don't know. Jonathan is still missing his wife. And I'm much younger than him. Sometimes I think he sees me as a bit of a nuisance."

"I doubt it. No one would ever see you as anything but a pleasure to be around."

Katie's cheeks blossomed from the compliment. "You're a *gut* friend, Anna, but I'm afraid what I say about Jonathan is true." With a sigh, Katie linked her arm through Anna's and guided her back to the kitchen door. "Jonathan Lundy isn't ready to begin again. When God blesses him with relief from his grief, then time will tell."

"That's good advice."

"Is it? Some days I forget what is good and what isn't. Some days I just long for things to move faster, or for guidance."

The stark words struck a chord within Anna. "I guess it's good we have so much to do, then," she said softly. "Otherwise, we'd be fretting all day."

Katie finally smiled. Bright and full of life and hope. "Anna, you are truly a gift to me. God bless you."

Anna hoped God would bless her with a great many things soon. Patience and hope and trust.

And parents who would one day go out of their way to help a daughter who really needed them.

Chapter 11

Katie did know best. After parting her hair down the middle, then fixing it neatly under her *kapp*, Anna realized with some surprise that over the time she'd been staying there, work, and the feeling of pride it had given her, had become important. It was also necessary to not forget that her work was needed. She was being asked to help because her efforts were important to the running of the inn, not just meaningless, made-up chores.

After receiving some instructions from Irene about how to go about oiling the oak furniture in the two west-wing bedrooms, Anna carried the bottle of oil and a pile of rags and got to work.

In no time at all, Anna cleared the utilitarian writing desk and dresser, then carefully poured a liberal amount of lemon-scented oil on the cloth and gently rubbed each piece of furniture.

She'd learned some time ago about the fine workmanship

and time that went into each table, dresser, and chair. Years ago, she and her mother had visited a farmers market and visited with an Amish man who spoke about the various steps he took in order to fashion a superior product.

Anna didn't know if she'd appreciated his patience at the time, or, for that matter, his pleasure in doing one task very well. She'd probably been in a hurry to get to the next stall or to investigate the quilts or, more likely to go home and see her friends and go to the mall.

But now all that seemed childish and foreign. Since first arriving at the Brennemans', the Plain clothes had begun to feel comfortable. The lack of time spent on vanity gave her freedom to pursue other interests. The lack of bombardment from a million vices gave Anna time to dwell on what was in her heart and mind. How strange it was to concentrate on her own goals and dreams instead of what everyone else thought she should do.

A burst of laughter floated upward. Curious, Anna peeked out the window. A woman stood in the parking lot, talking to Henry. She couldn't see much of the woman, her back was to the house, and the large oak in front of the house hindered much of the view from the window.

But she could see Henry. And he, for once, looked relaxed.

A stab of jealously filtered through her. Oh, not because he was speaking to another woman—but because it seemed that he was speaking so easily to her. Even their most earnest conversations had lately been stilted and full of tension.

When he glanced up toward the house, Anna turned away so he wouldn't catch sight of her. It wouldn't do for him to catch her spying.

But as his deep voice resonated through the air and seemed

to catch her heart and hold on. Why did each movement of his create a stir in her heart? Why was his furrowed brow a source of amusement instead of irritation?

She'd begun to think what they had between them was a relationship—something special to embrace, yet not defined, at least not defined in the way she used to characterize past relationships.

As she watched him, her hand barely moving the cloth around over the already polished woodwork, Anna dared to imagine that they had a future.

And for the first time, began to realistically imagine the consequences of such a thing.

Seeking solace, she turned from the window and breathed deep . . . and began to pray. God's will would be done.

Was she finally ready to listen?

"I'll be pleased to pass this on to Anna Metzger," Henry told the older woman who'd lumbered out of her shiny sedan and approached him in the parking lot. In clear, concise tones, she'd introduced herself as Mrs. Lowrey, a friend of Anna's parents. And then, before he could do any more than absorb the fact that Anna's parents had indeed heard Anna's phone call and had sent someone in their place, Mrs. Beverly Lowrey handed him a sealed envelope and announced that she'd be on her way.

Henry stepped in her path, effectively blocking the way to her car so he could claim some information. "I thank you for bringing it here."

"It was no bother, Mr. Brenneman. I care a lot for Meredith Metzger; I have since she became my neighbor thirty years ago. It was a pleasure to do something for her."

In spite of his efforts not to judge, for that was God's business, not his, Henry found he couldn't resist pointing out the obvious. "Mrs. Metzger wasn't able to come here herself? I think Anna would've liked to have seen her." Surely that was a fair understatement. Though she hadn't specifically shared her feelings of disappointment with him, Henry had seen the expression on her face when she'd spoken to Katie.

She'd been disappointed, which made him wish he had a way to ease her burdens.

If Mrs. Lowrey had personal feelings about her errand, she didn't look in any hurry to share them. Her tiny chin tilted a bit up as she replied. "She was 'able.' However, I don't believe she wanted to come this way. I'm assuming she had her reasons."

Henry wondered what they were. What kind of woman wouldn't rush to see her daughter the minute she knew she was hurting? "What would they have been, I wonder?"

"It wasn't my place to ask. Nor yours, either, Mr. Brenneman," she replied with more than a small hint of censure in her voice. "It would do us both a world of good to remember that, don't you think?"

"The Lord gave us a mind to wonder. I'm only doing that."

The lady's eyes remained piercing. "I learned over the years that it never pays to judge or to guess what other people are thinking."

"Or to criticize?"

After a pause, genuine amusement broke through her salty exterior. "Obviously, none of us is perfect."

"I'll take the letter to Anna."

"I'll tell her parents that I completed my errand, then." And with that, she turned and stepped to the left, making her way once more to her silver car. "As I said, this errand has been no trouble." She gestured to the wide fields behind them, one after another covered with a light dusting of snow. "This is pretty. I've always looked for an opportunity to visit Amish Country. I'm surprised it's taken me so long to come out this way."

"You should stay at our inn, then."

She cackled. "Ever the proprietor. Maybe I will one day soon. It's calming, even in the winter."

"Yes. Even in the winter."

Looking into the distance, she raised a hand to shield her eyes from the vibrant glow mirroring off the snow-covered fields. "I do have to admit that I got lost a time or two this afternoon. One must really want to visit the Brenneman Bed and Breakfast. If I hadn't promised Meredith I'd deliver this letter, I feel certain I would have abandoned this chore quite some time earlier."

Henry had heard that said more than a time or two. "The roads are marked, but winding. It takes time to learn their curves and hills and valleys, I'd say."

Mrs. Lowrey grinned. "It takes a bit more than time to learn this part of the county. It takes a good map and the patience of Job. I suggest you print out a better map for those of us who are not gifted with never-ending patience."

Henry couldn't help but appreciate her quip. Time and again, he'd ridden in folks' cars, directing them to the highway after their attempts had gotten them nothing but a half tank of gas. "Now that you're here, would you care to come in for a cup of tea or coffee?"

She looked longingly at the front of the house. As her gaze feasted on the wide-planked porch and the fine quartet of handmade rockers, Henry felt a burst of pride flow within him. He was proud of his home and their inn and always appreciated a newcomer's look of appreciation of his family's years of hard work.

"I'd enjoy a cup of coffee very much, but I'm afraid I have to get back. I promised to help out at the services at our church this evening, and as I said, getting here took a little longer than I expected."

"If you wait a moment, I will go get Anna for you. Perhaps you'd rather give her the note yourself, after all."

"There's no need." After a moment's hesitation, she reached out to him. "If you don't mind, though, please pass on a personal message from me."

"Gladly."

"Please tell Anna that I, for one, understand why she did what she did. It took more gumption than I can quite honestly say I ever thought she had in her left pinky to come here. She's done the right thing by my estimation."

He held up his hand and wiggled his fingers. "Left pinky. I will take care to remember that."

"Oh, enough of you," she said with an answering smile. "Just remember to tell her to stay strong and to do the right thing."

The words sounded cryptic. Henry was ready for more details—he needed more information if he was going to be able to help her at all. "Is she still in danger?"

"I don't know if I'd call it that, but I would tell you that her name has passed across a certain elected official's lips more than once, and he's not happy."

"Do you speak of Rob Peterson?"

"I do," Mrs. Lowrey said with a nod. "I've known Rob since

he was in short pants, and I'll tell you that I've never been more proud or flabbergasted by one man in all my days. He's a mass of contradictions, and the power he's obtaining has not served him well."

"What are you saying?"

"I'm saying that I, for one, can see why Anna might be afraid of him. I can understand how many others can be taken in by his easy smiles and effusive charm."

She stepped closer to her car and placed a gloved hand on the roof of it. "There are a lot of people depending on Rob now. He's made promises to important men in the state who are power hungry and ripe for abuses of power. They also believe in his leadership capabilities."

Her excuses sounded far-fetched to Henry. "They'll support such a man, even if they know he means to harm those closest to him?"

Mrs. Lowrey chuckled. "My boy, in my time I've seen men and women do a great many things for what they believe in. Don't get me wrong—some of those things were good, but not all. Like Isaac in the Good Book, men these days don't always do the right thing, and they don't always listen to what they should, either." Lifting her chin, she added, "And, those who follow men like Rob Peterson will believe a lot of lies if it means that they, too, will come out victorious. Sometimes victory is all that matters."

Henry found truth in her words. Even in their community, personalities clashed, and old hurts weren't always immediately forgiven and forgotten.

But that didn't mean he didn't trust Anna, and it didn't mean that she deserved any of what had happened to her.

Yes, the more he'd gotten to know Anna, the more he

was surprised that she'd been so taken in by a man like Rob. Yes, she had a flighty way about her, but she also seemed genuine and true. And gentle with a good heart. Speaking his mind, he said, "Why would a woman like Anna turn to a man like him?"

"I couldn't say, Mr. Brenneman. The same way we all turn to each other, I guess. Sometimes a person just has to trust in the Lord that the people in our paths are meant to be. If we didn't trust anyone, we'd have a very lonely life, now, wouldn't we?"

"I'd say you're right," Henry said quietly. All he had to do was think of Rachel to understand how life was full of surprises. He'd known Rachel all his life, had planned on a future much like his and her parents'. To his way of thinking, she'd wanted no different.

Only afterward had he discovered that she'd wanted far different things in life than he could ever offer, that she'd just kept her dreams hidden, blanketed under an agreeable nature in much the same way as ripe fields lay dormant under a covering of snow.

After another moment, Mrs. Lowery got back in her vehicle and pulled away, the wheels of her shiny white truck spitting rocks and gravel as she slowly drove down their lane and back onto the highway.

When there was silence again, Henry pocketed the letter and went to the barn. Now would not be the best time to hand Anna the letter. If he pulled her from the chores, it would disrupt her, and the rest of the afternoon.

No, it would be far better to give it to her at a moment when she would have time to quietly read and absorb her parents' note. Nothing done in haste ever came to much, he figured.

After checking on Stanley, Henry flexed his fingers to warm them up a bit, then began the repairs on one of the bedside tables he'd found gathering dust in the attic. With a lot of sanding, polish, and care, Henry felt sure he could restore the table to something of beauty and perhaps even sell it at the next market day.

He decided to pass on the letter to Anna after dinner. "May I have a word with you?" he asked as she helped to clear the table. Katie turned to him curiously, but he determinedly ignored her.

Anna's hands shook. "Um, all right," she said. "Let me just finish up here. Maybe in ten minutes or so?"

Henry nodded, hiding a smile. It was her way—her English way—to constantly refer to the time. So different than the Amish way of thinking, which focused more on chores and work to complete than how long each would take. "It's no hurry," he murmured. "I'll wait for you on the porch."

"On the porch? It's mighty cold out, Henry," Katie said. "Don'tcha think the hearth room would be far better?"

Anna kept her head down. "The porch is fine. I'm, uh, warm right now, and I'll put on a coat, too."

While Henry slipped on his own warm jacket, his father approached. Henry noticed that his father held a fresh branch off one of the oak trees and his whittling knife. Sometimes he carved beautiful canes out of the branches, and Henry sold them at the farmers market every now and then.

"Do I want to know what you are up to?" John asked.

"Probably not."

After checking to see that the swinging door was closed, his daed said, "Are you thinking of courting Anna?"

"No. This is about something far different." He'd wanted to give Anna the letter before sharing the news about the visitor with the rest of the family. It had only seemed right to give her that.

But, because his parents had a right to know what was going on, Henry sought to explain. "A lady came by this afternoon. She brought a letter to Anna from her parents. I want Anna to have some privacy when she reads it."

His father had the same reaction he'd had. "Why do you think her parents didn't come here themselves?"

"I don't know, though I will admit that their absence has brought Anna a fair share of grief. She misses them and needs their support."

"We all need support, I must say." Steepling his hands, his father added, "We all have the Almighty's support always, though. One needs only to ask."

"I hope Anna is doing that. I don't know if she is."

"Trust in the Lord with all thy heart, and lean not unto thine own understanding. In all thy ways acknowledge Him, and He shall direct thy paths."

The quote was a favorite of his father's. He'd quoted it from Proverbs often throughout the years. "Yes, *Daed*. You're right. As always."

That brought forth a fresh taste of laughter. "No, son, I'm not always right at all. But I am of strong enough mind to wish I was! And, to seek comfort and guidance where I might."

"It would serve me well to remember that."

"*Jah*, it would. Of course, you would also need to remember to give thanks for what you have every now and then, as well."

Henry knew where the gentle reminder had come from. Obviously his dissatisfaction with the way his life was had been noticed and discussed. In that, his father was correct, as well. It had been too long since he'd taken the time to give thanks for the things he had—his community, the wonderful world of nature that surrounded them. The opportunity to grow in a loving environment.

One day he would know who the Lord wished him to join with. He knew it as he knew the sun would come up in the morning. The sudden thought of green eyes and blond hair startled him. Was Anna that person? Could she ever be?

Stunned by the thought, he murmured, "*Danke*, Father."

"And thank you, son," his dad said quietly. "Your concern for Anna shows that you've grown up. Your newfound knowledge will serve you well, I am sure of it."

Henry wished he felt half so confident. As it was, his mind was awhirl with doing all he could to try to remember what was the right thing to do.

And since when had he ever struggled with that? He, who'd mistakenly prided himself on always knowing what was right. On knowing better than everyone else. Oh, yes, his pride had surely become his downfall.

Henry had a lot to think about as he put on his black felt hat and thick coat, and walked outside to wait for Anna.

The air was quiet and still. Tonight, it didn't seem as if even the animals felt like making their presence known. Above him, more stars than a man could ever care to count twinkled, offering hope that they'd get a break in the near constant rounds of snow they'd had lately.

Behind him, the door opened.

Like a woodpecker, his heart beat a little faster, calling on the rest of his body to take notice. Anna Metzger affected him like no other.

His father's words still fresh in his mind, Henry battled with his surprise. Was Anna his future?

"Henry? What did you want to discuss? Is anything wrong?"

He wanted to hold her hand and say nothing was wrong. That he had good news for her.

He wanted to take a risk and convey the awkwardness he felt around her. To share his feelings, his questions about her place in his life.

But he didn't dare.

Instead he did as he'd promised. "A woman came by today. Mrs. Beverly Lowery."

Anna swayed on her feet. "I saw you speaking with a woman, but I couldn't see her well from where I was. It was Mrs. Lowery?"

Because she looked to be on the verge of tears, Henry reached out and clasped her shoulders. Finally he escorted her to the pair of chairs in the back corner of the porch. The only spot, really, that wasn't visible from a window in their kitchen or hearth room.

"What did she want?" Anna finally asked. "Where is she?"

"She left soon after she arrived." He could wait no longer. Pulling out the white legal-sized envelope, he handed it to her. "She delivered this."

Anna set it on her lap like its temperature was so hot it

could singe her fingers. "That's my mother's handwriting on the envelope." Eyes wide, she looked at Henry. "What is going on?"

He had no earthly idea. And that, he realized as the verse from Proverbs floated into his mind once again, was exactly the point.

Chapter 12

Anna's hands shook as she held the paper.

Dear Anna,

If you are reading this letter, then Beverly must have made contact with the Brennemans and passed it on to you. For that, I am very grateful.

I can't tell you how relieved we were to hear your message on the machine. Your father and I have been beside ourselves with worry—we've had our doubts from the very beginning that you ever went to Florida. Why did you lie?

Anna cringed. Did they not remember her conversations with them? The way they'd ignored her when she asked for help?

Henry broke his silence. "Anna? You all right?"

"I'm fine." She just needed to remind herself that everyone

hadn't changed. Just because she had over the last month, it didn't mean that they had, too. With that in mind, she continued on.

> *Day after day, we've struggled to figure out what led you to deceive us about your whereabouts. To run, then go into hiding. However, as we've gotten to know Rob Peterson better, we realize there was much about him—and your relationship with him—that we never imagined. Now your father and I feel we understand what led you to run as you did.*

Anna scowled. "If they would have just listened to me before, I would have been so grateful."

"Perhaps you should wait a bit to continue?" Henry stood several feet away, his arms crossed over his chest. But his voice cast a soothing balm over her nerves. Gave her the strength to read more. To read more with an open mind.

"No, this needs to be done."

Perhaps wariness swam in her eyes because Henry, unbidden, stepped closer. "This letter is a *gut* thing, I'm thinkin'."

It was. She was coming to find out truth was always a good thing. Even when it was hard to come to terms with.

"Then what do we do?"

He pointed to the letter that was in danger of being crumpled in her hand. "Finish reading your parents' note."

Eyes burning, she skimmed to where she left off.

> *Anna, your father and I are going to investigate Rob's background more thoroughly. Though we think*

you should stay where you are, we want to continue to correspond. To work together with you to figure how to best free you from him.

We're smarter than we once were, Anna.

"I am too," she murmured.

For reasons we can't understand, Rob is determined to find you. He's searched your room more than once and has taken to following us around. That is why your father and I didn't go to the bed and breakfast to see you. Until we can find someone who is willing to stand up to Rob Peterson and help us, we are afraid to give any hint to where your location is.

Anna, please don't give up on us. Right now your father is meeting with a private investigator who knows everyone in the city. His father is a member of our church, and we feel certain we can trust him.

We will get to you—or send word—as soon as possible.

In the meantime, please know that you are in our thoughts and prayers and that we love you more than you'll ever know. Please continue to be brave, Anna.

Though many miles separate us, you are close in our hearts every waking minute.

Love, Mom

"There's nothing to forgive," she murmured, wishing with all her heart that her parents were there, beside her. "There's nothing to be ashamed of."

Saying those words aloud felt like she'd finally broken free from the last of her guilt. Forgiving her parents—and herself—buoyed her spirits and allowed her to begin to mend some of the many old hurts that had permeated her life of late.

Very slowly, Anna folded the letter back into thirds, then slipped it back into the envelope.

Minutes ran together as they sat on the porch, the cold wind biting their cheeks. She welcomed the sting. It made her feel more alive, stronger. Almost as if she could accomplish anything.

Henry broke the silence. "What did the rest of the letter say?"

"A lot. I'd appreciate it if you would read it, too."

"First, you tell me what you think."

How like Henry to encourage her to once again voice her feelings. "It was full of bad news," she reported, choosing to focus on her mother's words instead of how they made her feel. "Rob's been pestering them. Searching my room. My mother thinks he's been having them followed."

"There has to be some way they can break free of his wrath."

"My dad hired a private investigator. Well, he's talking with one."

She passed on the letter and Henry read it silently. To her surprise, when he finished and placed it back in the envelope, he guided her to one of the rocking chairs. She sat obediently.

Watched as he sat down beside her. And then . . . reached for her hand. To her surprise, she clung to his rough palm like a lifeline. Her pulse raced . . . though was it from the contact or from his empathy?

When their eyes met, he almost smiled. "You neglected to mention all the good parts."

That caught her off guard. "Were there any?"

"I'd say so." Gently, he murmured, "Did you not notice how many times she said she was sorry? Did you not notice how much they care? You haven't lost your parents, Anna." His voice roughened. "I'd venture to say that you've just found them once again. Anna Metzger, you are not alone at all. At the moment, you haven't ever been more surrounded by love and care. Anna, don't you see? You've never been more cared for."

At a loss for words, she focused on his hand in hers. On Henry's body next to hers. On how his strong build and assuring manner calmed her more than she ever thought possible. For whatever reason, she was tempted to lean on him.

With some surprise, she realized maybe she already had. Could that be the reason that she now sat with him so much instead of Katie? Because she needed him?

Or was it because he, too, had known abandonment and rejection? She knew Rachel's departure had hurt him very much. It was easier being open and honest with someone who'd also known heartache—who also knew what it was like to feel betrayed.

Finally she said, "You're right. I should be concentrating on the positives."

"It's difficult, though, isn't it?"

"It is because I don't know what to do. I feel trapped. Like I'm in a hole that's dug too deep to climb out of."

"You're forgetting that there are many ways to get out of such a place. You can build a ladder, ask for a rope, or hope someone will reach down and pull you up."

"I realize now that only with God's help can I get out," she murmured, shocking herself. "But I also know that you've been so helpful to me." She took a risk and met his gaze. "What happened to us, Henry? We used to not like each other."

"We opened our minds, I think."

She swallowed hard. "Sometimes I wish I wasn't going to leave one day."

A new emotion filled his gaze before he replied. "If you want to know the truth, sometimes I wish you wouldn't ever have to leave."

"If I stayed, I'd have to become Amish." To her surprise, the possibility wasn't overwhelming. On the contrary, it only sparked a flicker of curiosity.

What would it be like to become Amish? What would she be giving up?

More to the point, what would she be grabbing hold of?

Henry, as usual, had taken her question and pondered it carefully. "You would need to become Amish. But perhaps . . . it wouldn't be so difficult for you."

"You don't think so?"

He studied her more carefully. "Well, you already look like one of us."

As she spied the humor in his eyes, she laughed. And to her delight, he did, too. "Oh, Henry. I can't believe you're teasing me."

"You shouldn't be surprised. Everything canna be all so serious, Anna."

Their hands separated, and the thick band of tension that had hovered between them dissipated.

Folding her hands in her lap, Anna rocked back as the idea

of becoming Amish settled in. A thousand questions sprang forth. Would she even consider such a thing? She'd heard of people leaving the Amish, but never anyone who joined.

Henry rocked forward. "Anna—"

"Whatever are you two talking about in whispers?" Katie said from around the corner as she joined them on the porch. "It's cold enough out here to wish for an armful of thick goose-down blankets."

"Nothing," Anna lied before thinking.

Henry sprang to his feet. "*Jah*, we were just talking for a bit."

Within seconds, he excused himself, then disappeared into the barn, no doubt eager for the comfort of his work and animals.

For the first time since Anna had known her, Katie wasn't wearing an expression of tenderness and complete acceptance. Instead, she reminded Anna of a mother bear, angry and ready to defend her cub from any nasty intruder. "I've noticed over the last few days that you and my brother have become closer. At first I was mighty happy. The two of you had been at odds with each other since the time you met, and that tension certainly did weigh heavily on my mind."

Katie perched on the chair that Henry had just vacated. "But this . . . sitting in the dark—it is strange." Katie's eyes widened. "Is Henry courting you?"

Anna did her best to keep her expression neutral—not because she was about to laugh, but because she was afraid if she said a word tears would start running down her face.

However, Katie was still waiting for an answer. Anna decided to stick to facts. "You know we couldn't court, even if we wanted to."

"Because you are not Amish."

The earlier conversation with Henry floated closer, imprinted itself. "Exactly."

"But you fit in well now."

"That doesn't matter."

"Doesn't it?" With speculation, Katie eyed Anna with a shrewd expression. "You know much about the outside world, but I know about my brother and I know much about relationships."

Anna seriously doubted that but wisely held her tongue.

Rubbing her arms against the cold, Katie continued. "Perhaps our Lord didn't send you here to merely dress Plain. Maybe you came here in order to live with us and learn. Maybe living here, dressing Plain, adopting our ways . . . maybe it's how you were always intended to live."

Now Anna had no choice but to hold her ground. "Katie, you're making too much of things."

"I think not. Maybe it's time we discussed your future, don'tcha think?"

Unfortunately, Anna had no idea what to say now. So far, she'd had three people deliver far too many surprises. Too many to fully comprehend.

Rob decided to go out to the McClusky General Store himself. William Scott had contacted him again about his displeasure with his bachelor status, and though he'd tried, there was nothing that could ever happen between himself and Tracy. She was too stupid, too yielding, too vain.

The last time he'd taken her out to dinner, she'd worn a gown that had just barely covered her gorgeous figure. When she caused an outburst of attention, he'd caught her preening and enjoying the limelight. Taking the attention away from him.

She would never do.

When his brother-in-law still brought no news about Anna's whereabouts, Rob realized once again he was going to have to do everything himself. Even if he could find a woman to replace her, there was no way he could let her go out of his life without learning exactly how much she knew about his campaign finances. The election board was trying to make a name for itself by combing through each candidate's personal finances. Though he was fairly sure there were no trails showing just where he had spent the money, Rob sure wasn't going to risk the chance that Anna would come out of the woodwork and start talking nonsense about him.

To his left, a herd of cows mooed in a field whose fence was in serious need of repair. In the distance a man rode a horse, the man's hat identifying him as Amish.

Rob gripped the steering wheel of his Mercedes just a little bit harder, the action turning his knuckles white and igniting his temper all over again.

The Amish. Now there was a group of tax-evading backward folk. If he had his way, he'd put every one of them back into society and make them do their part for the economy.

How Anna could even think of associating with such people was beyond him.

After three wrong turns, Rob finally pulled into the lot of McClusky General Store. He parked off to the side, as far as possible from the buggies and horses situated near the entrance. The last thing he needed was a bunch of horse manure dirtying his wheels.

After stepping aside so two overweight women could

clamber down the steps, Rob pasted his "public" smile on his face and did his best to look genial.

The man behind the counter, dressed in an old flannel shirt and worn khakis, looked up when he approached. "May I help you?"

"Maybe." He held out a hand. "Rob Peterson. I'm running for U.S. Representative."

"Sam McClusky." The man shook his hand. "I'd say you're a far sight from home. Too far to be campaigning. And since the Amish don't vote, I'm wondering what your thinking is. What brings you out to these parts?"

Contrary to what the man looked to be, he obviously wasn't a fool. Rob tap-danced a reply. "Not too much. You know how the campaign life can be. So much pressure. Just thought I'd take the time and look around."

The proprietor's shoulders relaxed, though speculation still ran deep in his gaze. "Then this is a very good place to do that. Take your time."

When two men stood behind him, Rob stepped to the side and wondered again how he was going to find out anything.

He wandered the country store, which was an eclectic mix of old and new. Giant canisters of baking mixes and cereal were available for people to buy in bulk. On shelves in the back, kerosene lamps and boxes of candles were available for purchase.

Near the front was a vast selection of homemade canned vegetables and fruit. Apple butter and jars of cider kept company with spicy-looking relishes and pickle spears.

The store wasn't especially crowded. An Amish family was near the baked goods, two daughters who couldn't be much over eight were dressed exactly like their mother. A couple of tourists were talking to the owner now. He was giving them directions to some inn.

When the other man caught his eye, Rob knew he had to either buy something fast or leave. On a whim, he picked up three jars of honey, thinking the jars a fitting purchase since he was about to be sweeter than he'd ever been.

"That all?"

"It is. These are going to make nice gifts."

"They will indeed. Nothing like the taste of homegrown honey."

Rob pulled out a pair of tens and handed them over. "Where might a guy go to relax around here?"

The elder man's mustache twitched. "To relax, hmm? Depends what you want to do, I'd reckon."

"Nothing too out of the ordinary. Sit around, sip a cup of coffee. Learn more about the people out here." Even Rob knew he didn't sound convincing. Passing over a better smile, he added, "I'm really interested in the folks around here. Any chance these Amish will accept strangers in their midst?"

"You interested in becoming Plain?"

Rob was a seasoned politician, and he knew exactly when to tell the truth and when to lie through his teeth. It was the time to tread carefully here. "Not in this lifetime. But I am interested in what might drive a person to leave society to do such a thing. Have you ever heard of anyone doing that? Becoming Amish?"

"No."

"Come on," he prodded, his voice heavy on the Karo syrup. "No one new ever comes and stays awhile?"

"I didn't say that." McClusky eyed him a little more closely, obviously trying to read his mind.

Rob let him look his share. He was used to people trying to figure him out. What they didn't realize was that he could do the same thing a whole lot better. He'd gotten far in life telling people what they wanted to hear. And they all wanted to hear something—every last one.

Carefully putting the honey in a paper sack, McClusky continued. "Well, like anyone else, the Amish have relatives from all over. Some have moved away in order to buy more land. Lots have moved here to Ohio from Pennsylvania way. Land is expensive to purchase."

"Have you seen any new to the area lately?"

"No."

Rob pulled out three hundred-dollar bills. Setting them on the counter in between them, the crisp bills practically begged to be picked up. "Are you sure you haven't seen a woman here, new to the area? She has beautiful green eyes. Very unusual."

The man's expression became a blank mask. "I don't know what you are looking for, but you won't find it here." He pushed the Benjamins back to Rob. "It's time you left."

Recognition had flickered in McClusky's expression when he had mentioned green eyes. He knew something, Rob was sure of it. Fun and games are over. "My fiancée ran away. Her name's Anna Metzger. Her parents are frantic for her. We think she got involved in drugs. She might even have brought her dealer or her supply into this county. She's dangerous. If you see her, contact me. Or better yet, contact Sheriff Grant." Rob passed over another card. "You'd hate a woman like that tainting anything here in God's country. You'd hate to be blamed for a whole community's ruin because you couldn't stand the truth. Because you refused to tell the truth." Lowering his voice to a whisper, Rob said, "I know I'm right."

"Go. Now."

"I will, but I'm coming back." Rob left the bills on the counter and walked off. But inside he felt triumphant. The man had seen Anna.

Finally, finally, he was on the right track. In no time, he'd get Anna, Scott would get off his back, and things would be back to normal.

Chapter 13

Katie had been unnaturally quiet all day. Well, that wasn't exactly true, Anna allowed. Katie had been quiet around her, and her alone.

Anna wondered what she'd done, exactly, that had made her friend so standoffish. The conversation the night before about Henry and adopting the Amish way of life? Perhaps it had more to do with her continued presence at the bed and breakfast, taking up space and getting in the way. Though Katie had been nothing but gracious, she was also human. It was only natural to be tired of a houseguest.

After Anna finished drying the last of the platters from breakfast and put them away, she decided to go find out what she could do to make things better. Anna was well aware of her flaws, and they included being unable to wait for others to come to her. She couldn't handle Katie's cold shoulder.

And, if she'd learned anything over the last month, it was that hiding true, honest feelings was never a good thing.

She found Katie in the hearth room, attaching a collar to a shirt. Beside her was a basket of quilt fabrics for her Center Diamond quilt. The carefully cut pieces of black, cherry red, evergreen, and cobalt blue regally waited to be stitched together. "Hi."

Katie barely looked up. "Hello, Anna."

Though she hadn't been invited, she approached and sat down next to her. "You've been avoiding me all day, Katie. Why?"

Blue eyes widened as she neatly tucked the needle into the fabric. "Why would you ask such a thing?"

"Because you haven't seemed yourself." Anna felt like pointing to the fabric currently getting scrunched under Katie's usually nimble hands. Anyone who knew Katie would realize such behavior was out of character. "I'm worried you're upset with me."

"That's not true." After carefully smoothing out the fabric, Katie pushed the needle through the cloth once again.

"All right." Anna tried to believe Katie, but she didn't at all. Katie's expression and tone screamed uneasiness. "Would you tell me if you were troubled?"

"Of course I would."

"Okay. Well, I'll leave you alone, then," Anna said, afraid to push any harder.

Just as she stood to walk away, Katie tossed the shirt on the table. "I'm mighty *naerfich* nervous about your relationship with my brother Henry," she blurted.

There was only one thing Anna could say. "I know you are."

"You're not going to deny what I've seen?"

"No." Anna owed Katie that much . . . though truthfully, she didn't know what had been going on between the two of them. Not really.

Katie raised her head. "Henry's already had his *rumschpringe*. Did he tell you that? He is not eager to live among the English again."

"I know. Once more, I have no desire to make him leave you or your family. This community is where he belongs—anyone could see that."

"Anyone?"

Katie's posture was like a mother cub defending her own. Anna wondered just how many other people knew that Katie Brenneman was far stronger than most would ever imagine! "Anyone," Anna repeated. "Even me."

"Then you should leave him alone."

"Katie, I'm not a scarlet woman attempting to draw him from all he holds near and dear!"

"I do know that you've been a mite too forward with him. His eyes have strayed."

"I can't help that."

"Of course you can. We all can control our desires for the sake of living peacefully together." Chin up, Katie said, "Surely you wouldn't disagree?"

Quickly, Anna looked to the door, afraid someone would overhear them. Then she attempted to explain herself. "Everything that has happened between Henry and me has been mutual. I think he's enjoyed my company as much as I've enjoyed his. But we're just friends. Don't you see?"

"No. I am sorry, but I do not. I see a light that shines in his eyes when he sees you. Whenever you enter the room. He's hurting from Rachel, don'tcha see?"

"I'm not Rachel, and I'm not responsible for his past hurts. Can't you imagine what I'm going through? I've been hiding out for weeks here. Taking your hospitality. Worried about my parents. Worried that I've brought it all on you."

"But you're still here."

There it was. "Are you asking me to leave?"

A stricken expression entered Katie's face, but she didn't reply. Because in the doorway was Irene Brenneman.

"Whatever is going on here, girls?"

"We're merely having a discussion," Katie mumbled.

Irene raised a brow. "And quite a discussion, too, I'd say. Anna, dear, what's this I heard about you thinking it's time to leave?"

Katie's face went white as Anna hastily sat back down. She didn't know what to say. Already too much had been spoken aloud, perhaps she should now just say nothing.

With a guilty look toward Anna, Katie spoke. "Her leaving would be my doing, *Mamm*. I know she's turned Henry's head and it's not fair."

Irene looked from Anna to Katie, then finally clasped her hands together and nodded slowly. "Yes, I can see how you would worry about our Henry . . . seeing how he has no mind of his own."

If she'd intended for the words to have shock value, Anna thought Irene Brenneman had hit pay dirt. Both her head and Katie's had snapped to attention so hard she was surprised neither of them was complaining of whiplash.

"Anna, I, too, have seen the way Henry has watched you. Have you not?"

"There's a connection between us that is hard to deny," Anna admitted, "But I promise I'm not trying to hurt him.

Or any of you." With all her heart, she wanted to repeat the conversation they'd shared the night before, but she didn't dare. Henry was too private to embarrass him that way. It was also his place to speak to his family, not hers.

"You would hurt us all if he left the order to be with you," Irene agreed. "We'd deeply regret that, though we wouldn't try to stop him."

With a look of wonder at her mother, Katie whispered, "You wouldn't try?"

"You can't force a person to believe something they don't— just like you can't make someone *lieb* you if they don't."

Katie folded her hands across her chest. "I'm learning that myself."

"There's really only one thing to do if you and Henry are really fit for each other," Irene said, her words sounding as if they came from deep within her heart, from a place where only true feelings lay and honest emotions reigned.

And that made Anna nervous. "What is that?"

"You could join us, dear Anna. You . . . could become Amish."

Three conversations in three days. It was time to open her heart and listen to what the Lord was asking her to do. Was it to stay?

Or was it to go back where she came from and try to un- ravel the relationships with her parents and friends?

Both choices sounded difficult and hard to accomplish.

"I feel ridiculous," Calvin said as they pulled out of the En- terprise Rental Car lot. "Meredith, we have no idea what we're doing."

Meredith privately agreed, but didn't voice her opinions.

"Calvin, all we're doing is taking every necessary precaution."

"Every necessary precaution involves buckling seat belts and making sure we have enough gasoline. What you've reduced us to is mind boggling."

That was true, but it was also true that they were out of options. The initial meeting with a private investigator had been eye-opening. He'd made it clear that it would be virtually impossible to check on Anna unnoticed, and he also detailed the extremely dangerous job it would be to tail someone of Rob Peterson's wealth and influence.

All of it also sounded extremely expensive with few guarantees of learning more than what they already knew.

After much discussion, they decided to go retrieve Anna themselves. They'd waited long enough, and things weren't about to get any easier.

So they rented a car and bought some frumpy-looking clothes. Now they didn't look Plain or even like Mennonites, but Meredith had a feeling that one of their acquaintances might walk past them before taking a closer examination.

She sure didn't recognize herself. For the first time since she'd become a teenager, she wasn't wearing any makeup. Instead of styling her hair and curling it, she'd left it to dry naturally, then tied it into a small ponytail at the nape of her neck.

Instead of her usual bright pinks and reds, she wore a modestly cut chambray blue blouse, neatly tucked into an ankle-length skirt. Loafers and a thick black coat completed her outfit.

As for Calvin, his slacks and shirt looked like any in his closet. But his shoes were sturdy instead of designer and his coat was serviceable and thick.

Gone were the contacts he'd worn for the last fifteen years. In their place were thick glasses. The wire rims changed his appearance more than anything, bringing a casual observer's eye to the lines around his lips and eyes.

"We look older. A lot older." Meredith had to smile—for the first time in her life, she had made getting older sound like a good thing!

Calvin grimaced. "At this moment, I certainly feel older. I feel like we've aged ten years over the last month." As they headed up I-75, he shook his head. "What if we're followed?"

"I think that's a chance we're going to have to take. Anna needs us, and we need her."

"If we bring Rob to the Brennemans, I won't be able to forgive myself."

Meredith frowned. "I already can't forgive myself. This will just add to our list of problems. All I do know is that if Rob finds her before we even take a risk—well, that would be even harder to bear."

The skies turned dark, making the February afternoon seem more gloomy than usual. "Snow's on the way," Henry stated with a frown. "I best go prepare the parking lot and make sure we have plenty of wood for the fireplace."

"I'll see what your mom would like me to do," Anna said through her haze. Sometime during the night before, the cold and stress had compounded and given her a doozy of a head cold. Now it felt like she had weights settling on her sinuses and enough aches and pains to feel like she'd gone five rounds in the boxing ring.

With a wry smile, Henry patted her shoulder. "Perhaps

you should consider resting instead, Anna. You don't look too well."

His criticism stung, though she knew he was absolutely right. She didn't look well. Vanity kicked in for the moment, and she wished she had a bit of makeup to cover the dark circles under her eyes or a bit of powder to hide some of the redness of her nose. "I hate not to do my part."

"You would end up not doing your part if you continue as you are right now. Our guests probably wouldn't fancy their meals served by a sickly Amish lady." A teasing smile lit his eyes. "I don't know why."

Anna refrained from saying another word to that, because she knew he was absolutely right. With a sigh, she sat back down on the rocker in the hearth room. Carefully, she pinned a black rectangle to the main square that would serve as the focal point for the whole quilt. As usual, the painstaking work brought her joy—she truly enjoyed piecing together the bits of cloth, to make a beautiful creation out of scraps of leftover fabric.

Anna also used the time to wonder what the future had in store for her. Around her, she heard the handful of guests talking in the parlor as they prepared to go for a hike in the wooded trails before the snow started falling.

In the kitchen, Mrs. Brenneman had two lady friends over. They were making potato casseroles for the inn and for a family whose daughter was sick and in the hospital. Above her, Katie was bustling as good-naturedly as ever in one of the guest rooms.

And with some surprise, Anna realized that she fit in. Not just because she blended in and no longer looked like a fancy girl. No, she fit in because she appreciated the way of life, and appreciated her role in the household. Before her bout with the flu, she had done her part to help with the inn.

Time and again, Irene had praised her work ethic, which was high praise indeed, for the Amish were notoriously hard workers and not given to handing out compliments for things expected.

What was going to happen with her and Henry? Was he her future? How had their rocky relationship turned into something far different? Something special and fulfilling? Now, she caught herself admiring his capable ways. Admired his blunt way of speaking. Appreciated the way his shoulders were broad and how his gentle ways meshed nicely with his very handsome looks.

She'd felt a tingling of awareness when their eyes caught sight of each other. When they both forgot to look away and allowed a bit of heat and interest to spark.

Was this how it was meant to be?

Not for the first time, Anna wondered if the Lord had guided her to the Brennemans. Oh, she'd gone at first for selfish reasons, to seek refuge in the one place she knew she would be safe. But since then, she'd traded much of her selfish and lazy ways for a more productive and giving nature.

No, it hadn't been easy. But wasn't the Bible full of stories of average men and women who didn't always listen to God the first time? Who needed to be reminded time and again to pay heed to His signs?

Could she leave her old life? Could she leave the modern necessities? The hectic lifestyle she'd thought she'd thrived on, the trips and worldly possessions she'd always thought she needed?

But more important, could she adopt the Amish way

of life, the true way of life, in which religion wasn't just a Sunday activity but something that intertwined through every day, through every waking moment?

She rocked some more. Threaded a needle and began to stitch. Worried about impulsivity. Worried about making a quick decision based on all the wrong things.

Was she suddenly excited about the change in lifestyle because she'd discovered that there'd been a whole other life hidden in her heart, just waiting to be recognized and nurtured?

Or was she still seeking refuge from Rob and from the disappointment in her relationship with her parents and the lack of success in the outside world?

That thought brought her up short. Was she really that shallow?

Days ago, she would have said yes. Of course, days ago—a mere month ago, she wouldn't have taken the time to reflect. No, she would have only concentrated on the things she wanted and the things she couldn't have, never mind the consequences. Yep, she'd been very good at that.

As the flames flickered in the fireplace in front of her, she allowed her eyes to drift shut. At the same time, Anna allowed her mind to relax and feel the guiding hand of the Lord nurture her.

And feel it she did. At once she felt peace and compassion—not just for others, but for herself. Perhaps that was what she'd needed? To accept herself and all her faults . . . but to also accept that she wasn't all bad. That she had a lot of worthwhile qualities?

* * *

"Anna? Anna wake up," Katie said from the doorway.

She struggled to focus her groggy brain. "I'm sorry, I must've fallen asleep. Do you need help? I can go—"

"No, Anna, it's something else." Worriedly, Katie stepped from one foot to the other, as if she wasn't sure whether to join Anna in the hearth room or to encourage her to get up and leave.

Truly curious now, Anna stood up and hastily folded the quilt. "What's wrong?"

Katie's expression turned miserable. "You have visitors, Anna."

The words hit her like a sledgehammer, just as she turned to the doorway and gasped.

Chapter 14

It took a moment, but Anna found her voice. However, what she spoke was far from earth shattering. "You came."

"We did." Flashing a smile, her mother stepped forward. "We couldn't stay away another minute, even if coming here was dangerous."

"We've been so worried about you, Anna," her father added.

"I know." But, really . . . did she?

Anna supposed she should feel compelled to run into their arms. To reclaim everything between she and her parents that she'd thought she lost.

But instead, she stood staring at them . . . just as they did her. They looked nothing like their familiar selves. Her mother was always perfectly coifed and made-up. So much so that Anna had once compared her to a doll to her friend

Julie when they were teenagers. Now, though, her mother's drab, shapeless clothes made her look every bit of her fifty-some-odd years.

Her dad's glasses magnified the wrinkles around his eyes. And, had he always had so much gray hair at his temples?

Or, maybe their awkwardness had very little to do with outfits and everything to do with the circumstances of the situation. Never had Anna imagined that she would be dressed Plain, hiding out from an abusive congressional candidate in an Amish bed and breakfast.

Poor Katie darted worried looks her way and wrung her hands. Henry appeared, guided them all into the room, then offered his hand. "I am Henry Brenneman."

Her dad·shook it. "Calvin Metzger. This is my wife, Meredith."

They were all speaking to each other so formally. So businesslike. Not like her parents usually spoke to her. Not like Henry usually did. And she was the worst of all, Anna realized. She knew everyone. Had depended on each person at one time or another. And still, there she stood, as motionless as that hare in the meadow she and Henry had once spied.

Henry continued the social graces as if he was accustomed to doing such things every day. "And this here is my sister, Katie."

Her mother nodded in Katie's direction. "We . . . we know each other. From when Anna took that quilting class." Anna noticed that still her mother hadn't taken her eyes off her.

Of course, Anna hadn't been able to look away, either.

Always proper, Katie cleared her throat. "Anna, are you all right?"

A month ago she would have smiled and said she was. A day ago she would have said everything was not all right, and maybe would never be that way again.

But as of right that minute, Anna couldn't really say how she was feeling. Words garbled in her brain as her two worlds collided—her past, filled with missed opportunities and an aimlessness she couldn't escape. Her life with the Brennemans, filled with hard work, a loving, bustling family, and Henry.

Henry!

She took a deep breath; let His sense of peace flow through her. Suddenly, everything became very clear. It was time to step forward into her new life, and accept all the challenges that came with it. It was time to stop hiding.

Her dad's tone turned stern. "Anna, what is wrong with you? Katie just asked you a question."

"No, I'm not all right."

Her mother swayed and reached out for her father. Katie inhaled quickly.

Only Henry looked her way in understanding. Only Henry wrapped his hand around her shoulder. Touching her in a way that made her realize she wasn't alone. Not here. Not in her heart. She had him, and even more important, she had God's guiding hand.

For a moment, she met his gaze. In his eyes, she saw acceptance and pride. Hope and . . . love?

She tried again. "I mean. I'm not okay but I think I will be." Stepping forward, she reached out for her parents just as Henry's hand fell from her shoulder, leaving a cool imprint of loss.

"Perhaps Katie and I should leave you," he said. "Or would you rather I stay, Anna?"

It wasn't a hard question. As a matter of fact, it really shouldn't matter at all, whether he stay or go. But for the life of her, it felt like a monumental decision was about to take place. "Please stay."

Her father frowned. "Honestly, Anna—"

Henry interrupted. "Mr. and Mrs. Metzger, I think I'll be staying, if you two don't mind."

Her dad looked like he did mind, very much. His eyes narrowed as Henry's hand reached for her hand, showing all of them that there was more to their relationship than any of them might have ever suspected.

As Katie slipped out of the room, Meredith broke into a strained grin. "That's fine. Fine."

Henry took the lead. "Perhaps we should all sit down." Once again, his hand was a guiding force, gently propelling her to a chair. Her parents sat across from them, in the love seat John and Irene Brenneman enjoyed so much. Henry took a seat in an oak ladder-back chair.

For better or worse, Anna needed to hold herself accountable and be ready to face the consequences, even overwhelming ones. Yet, she also couldn't hide or withhold her feelings. She'd spent too many evenings in the quiet of her room, with only her thoughts for company as she worked on her Diamond Square quilt. During those quiet times, she'd dwelled on a lifetime of things she wished she could change. On a lifetime of things she wished were different. Of her faults and her weaknesses.

However, she knew it was a mistake to claim all responsibility. Rob was at fault, too.

But she also harbored resentment toward her parents. And though she could forgive their actions, she also knew she would never forgive herself if she didn't vocalize some of her feelings. "I didn't think you were coming. I didn't think you cared."

"We did." Calvin visibly choked out the words. "You know we care about you, Anna. We always have."

Then why did they try so hard to disguise their feelings all the time? "Your letter said that you couldn't get away."

"Our letter said we didn't dare try and come here," her mother corrected. "However, it didn't change what was in our hearts. And it couldn't change the very fact that we love you and miss you."

Though she didn't contradict their words, Anna knew that her feelings showed through her expression. And no matter how hard she tried to pretend otherwise, she couldn't help herself. In short, she had needed their support and understanding, and the evening before she'd left for the Brennemans', they'd been anything but supportive of her.

By her side, Henry said nothing, but she felt him stiffen. She knew what he thought—that it was time to practice forgiveness. To feel for them and to bear in mind that this whole experience hadn't been easy for anyone involved.

Quietly, her father spoke. "Anna, I know you don't want to believe us because we certainly haven't been there for you in the past. That's something we can't change, no matter how much we would like to do so."

Leaning forward, Meredith said, "I am sorry, Anna. If I could turn back time, I would."

Her mother's words shamed her, and brought her out of her pity party.

Hadn't she planned to show them and herself just how far she'd come from the self-centered person she'd once been?

How easy it would be to let them shoulder all the blame! Let them shoulder everything, and let herself pretend she was completely innocent.

But sometime in between the afternoon she'd knocked on the door and now, Anna knew she'd grown up. She'd matured into the type of woman who put others before herself. Who was able to face the truth even when the truth wasn't good at all. "I'm sorry, too. I know I've worried you," she said quietly.

"Even though it may not seem like it, we've been on your side."

"You've been there for me time and time again."

"Not when you needed us most."

After receiving an encouraging nod from Henry, Anna said, "Living here, living this way, being with the Brennemans— well, it's given me time to think. A lot of time to think."

"Much to all of our dismay," Henry said, surprising them all with a much-needed bit of levity.

Anna smiled. "I think everything happened for a reason. The life I was living wasn't a good one, Mom."

Meredith held up a hand, and Anna waved her off. "Mom, I know you like Rob, but he's dangerous. Yes, his friends are influential and not all of them are bad. But *he* was. He was controlling and wrong." She couldn't bear to say abusive. She didn't want to place that burden on her parents' shoulders.

"We don't think he's the one for you anymore," her dad said.

"Actually, we found out pretty quickly there were a lot of things about him that we didn't want to see. A lot of things hidden under his very handsome face and shiny personality." Meredith fought a shiver. "He came to the house. Several times, actually. When he searched your room, he took a bunch of your photo albums."

Anna could barely get her arms around the idea that Rob had not only been in her room, but had rifled through her belongings. "I wonder why he took the albums. Did he say why?"

"He didn't give us very many explanations, Anna, and the explanations he did give hardly made sense." Scooting to the end of the sofa, Meredith looked first at Henry, then met Anna's gaze. "But one thing I know for certain is that he's determined to find you, Anna. He's so determined that he's stopped over time and again."

"And each time he's spoken to us, he's become more angry and threatening," her father finished. "This is beyond a need to see you . . . he's become a desperate man."

"I knew he was becoming more violent. I just didn't know how to stop him."

"I don't know if you could have. He seems to be on his own path . . . and each time we've talked with him, he's surer than ever that we're hiding you and keeping you from him."

"We had begun to worry that he was just putting on an act, that maybe he'd done something with you, or that you'd injured yourself or come to real harm hiding from him."

Meredith blinked back tears. "Thank goodness Miriam saw you."

"I guess you realized I wasn't in Florida right away?"

"Only after we talked to Rob the first time. That's when I went in your room and did some checking on my own."

"Your mother's been calling old friends, too."

Thinking of the many people she'd pushed away . . . not

wanting to deal with Rob's wrath, Anna swallowed hard. "Did you speak to anyone?"

"We talked to a lot of people. The most illuminating was Julie."

Julie. Her old friend whom Anna had practically abandoned. "I'm surprised she didn't hang up on you when she found out why you called. I haven't been very good to her."

"She was worried about you."

"We think Rob is close to locating you."

Henry leaned forward. "You think he knows Anna's here?"

"I do. Someone told us he went to the McClusky General Store. There is a very good chance someone there might have given your location away."

"That could have happened," Henry said. "This is a close-knit community, for sure."

He had found her. The room began to spin. Once again, Henry came to her rescue, wrapping an arm around her shoulders.

"Anna?" he murmured in her ear, holding her close. "Anna, you okay?"

She reached out for him, she couldn't help it. Henry Brenneman was the antithesis of Rob. In her mind, he'd become a symbol of what was good and decent in the world, and she needed that, and him, desperately.

When she noticed her parents watching her in alarm, Anna attempted to explain. "I'm sorry . . . it's just that I've been in the store."

"Don't you think that was foolish, Anna?" her dad asked. "If you were trying to hide, like you said, you should have stayed hidden."

"Anna going to McClusky's wasna all that unusual, to my thinking," Henry explained. "All of us Amish shop there." Anna liked how he included her in the grouping. Her father must have noticed it, too, because he widened his eyes, though he said nothing more.

"I can't believe I could have run into him." A shudder coursed through her at the thought. "I don't know what I would have done if that had happened."

"But it didn't, did it?" Henry said softly. "Do not be so hard on yourself, Anna. Don't borrow trouble."

His words and his kindness gave her comfort. "I'll try not to."

Hoping to lighten up the conversation, she pointed to the worn chambray shirt and ugly beige skirt her mother was wearing. If she hadn't been so shocked to see her parents, she would have asked her mom right away how she had managed to pick out something that was so very unflattering. "So, Mom, what's with the outfit?"

Meredith chuckled. "Well . . . you know how I usually dress. I thought maybe my usual attire of pants and bright pink sweater might be a little much."

"So you thought to blend in?"

Anna chuckled. Even Henry was getting into the teasing mode. Everything was going to be okay! "Mom, you could blend in with an oak tree . . . that skirt is so big and flowy."

Her dad chuckled. "You'd never believe it, but we did try to be inconspicuous."

"And sneaky," her mother added.

"Well, as sneaky as we could possibly be. We rented a car and tried to disguise ourselves. Mainly, we hoped we just wouldn't be instantly recognizable. Or instantly remembered for standing out," her mom said.

"We were also afraid Rob would follow us."

Anna was touched and genuinely surprised. "You do care."

"Of course we care. We love you, Anna."

The words felt good. They were so needed. So very needed and helped fill a gap in her heart that had been forced open. Standing up, she ran to her mother and knelt in front of her, wrapping her arms around her mom's waist, just like she used to do when she was small.

Her mother automatically curved her arms around Anna and patted her back. "Please don't worry anymore. Please don't worry, Anna. Everything's going to be okay."

For the first time in a long time, Anna dared to think that, too.

Nothing was going right. Nothing was going according to plan. Rob Peterson closed his eyes against the pounding headache, just as Omar the taxi driver took a turn too quickly and Rob practically slid across the backseat. "Watch it!" he snapped.

"You said you were in a hurry. I'm getting you to your place as quickly as possible."

"I want to be in one piece, though." He also didn't want to attract attention. Though he had no doubt he could talk his way out of any situation, explaining his presence in the back of a taxi in the middle of Amish country might be stretching things a bit far.

Rob held on as the driver flew over a deep ridge in the road, then braked quickly in order not to charge into a horse and buggy. The horse neighed and the woman driving stared at them in alarm.

"Hey!" Rob yelled. "You're going to kill somebody if you don't watch out."

Omar met his eyes in the rearview mirror. "Relax, mister. I'm not about to kill anyone today."

Today? A chill rushed down Rob's spine that had nothing to do with the frigid temperatures seeping through the ramshackle vehicle and everything to do with a strong sense of foreboding. Omar seemed unstable. It was a mistake to pay him a thousand dollars to make the trip. He should have found another way to get to Anna. As they zipped past yet another yellow sign emblazoned with a horse and buggy on it, Rob tightened his seat belt and attempted to put his mind on something else. Anything else.

Just as he'd been about to buy a tourist map and start knocking on doors to look for Anna, his worthless brother-in-law had come through. After two weeks of questioning, Grant had found the taxi driver who'd run Anna up to Amish country. And once more, he'd threatened his green card so well that Omar was willing to do just about anything to make sure he could keep his job. Well, anything that involved being paid a grand or two.

Rob was really grateful for the recent windfall of campaign contributions, otherwise he would have had to dig into his savings account to pay off Omar.

As they practically skidded to a stop at a stop sign next to a plain white clapboard house, Rob snapped, "How much longer?"

"Ten minutes. More or less."

Rob rolled his eyes, then gripped the seat again as Omar

pulled out into the intersection and sped past yet another buggy, this one carrying an Amish lady and three little girls. All three wore violet dresses, black capes, and black bonnets. He might have found the sight touching if not for the fact that each one of them reminded Rob of what he'd lost.

Correction. Almost lost.

He bit back the impulse to ask again how much longer the ride would be, fearing Omar would joke about him sounding like a child on a car trip.

"It's pretty here, don't you think?" Omar murmured.

"If you like snow-covered corn fields."

"Ah, but in the summer, the sights are far different. Knee high by the Fourth of July, right?"

"That's what they say," Rob replied, wondering how on earth the guy knew such a quaint expression.

Then, just when Rob couldn't take another minute of their joyride, Omar slowed. "This is it," he said, slowing the car down.

Rob peered out the window. There, in all its glory, stood a neatly painted oak sign, with the words *Brenneman Bed and Breakfast* carved in block letters. "This has to be it."

Omar swung onto the gray graveled road, taking no heed that rocks flew around them like fireflies in the summer. Stones sprayed the windshield, but Omar didn't seem to mind.

The road leading up to the house seemed about a mile long. In the distance, a large two-story building neatly trimmed in black awaited them. The front porch held four large white rocking chairs.

On a clothesline in the back hung two navy-colored dresses and one bright red, black, and orange quilt.

"This is a nice place," Omar observed. "I remember seeing a pair of black horses last time I was here."

The guy acted like that would be a quite a sight. Hadn't he noticed the horses he'd just about run over? "Whatever," Rob murmured, glancing at his watch. "Park over by the side, in that parking lot, but don't go anywhere."

"Where would I go?" For the first time, Omar's pleasant expression wasn't so pleasant. In fact, it looked almost . . . resentful. Full of animosity.

A prickle of distrust hit Rob hard. Just how desperate was this guy? Desperate enough to go against him even though he'd pocketed half of his money? "Just be ready. I'm going to have a woman with me."

"How long is this going to take?"

With any luck, no time at all. But so far, things hadn't been so lucky at all. "Thirty minutes, tops."

"If it's over an hour, I'm going to charge you double."

The guy was such an idiot. Did he really think Rob was going to give him any more than he already had? "If it's over an hour, you can shoot me," Rob joked. "There's no way I want to be here longer than I have to."

Tires crunched as Omar pulled into the parking lot. On the far side, a black-and-white cow stared at them in interest. Rob hardly spared it a glance. As soon as the car stopped, he opened his door and got out, cold air making his eyes water for the first few seconds.

Right away the smell of manure, cows, and horses surrounded him. A chicken or turkey or something squawked a welcome. Quickly Rob checked his Italian loafers. The last thing he wanted was to step in something and ruin the expensive leather.

Buttoning his overcoat, he was finally about to do what he'd been trying to do for the last month: retrieve Anna.

From behind him, Omar stepped out of the taxi and leaned up against it. A second later, the sweet smell of a cigar floated forward.

As Rob stomped along, taking care to avoid icy slick spots that hadn't been shoveled all that well, it hit him that Omar hadn't laughed at his joke. On the contrary, he acted like he might just have a gun . . . and that he knew how to use it.

Once again, Rob cursed Anna Metzger. She was going to pay for this episode. She was going to pay if it was the last thing he—or Omar—ever did.

Chapter 15

"Excuse me, ma'am. I'm looking for Anna Meztger. Is she here?"

The words carried all the way from the front entryway into the hearth room where Anna, Henry, and her parents sat. Even from that distance, Anna knew the voice.

Rob Peterson had found her.

Across from Anna, her mother stiffened. "Calvin, get up! We've got to do something."

Dutifully, Calvin stood up. Henry did, as well. But Anna knew it was time for her to step forward. "I'll go talk to him," she said, rising from the couch.

Her mother reached for her hand. "Anna, you will do no such thing. Sit back down and stay here."

"No, Mom. He came to see me."

Calvin scowled. "Don't be foolish."

"I'm not being foolish at all," Anna protested mildly. "This is what I need to do." For the first time since she'd gone into hiding, Anna didn't fear Rob or what the future might bring.

Perhaps she'd finally grown up.

But more likely, Anna thought it was that she'd found quite a bit while hiding from Rob. She'd discovered an old friend in Katie. She'd tested and pushed the boundaries of love with her parents and had realized that there was a stronger connection than she'd ever given credence to.

With Henry, she'd discovered love can come slowly, patiently, and not be the by-product of fierce passion and whispered promises, but by the steady security in knowing you are valued as a complete, whole child of God.

Truthfully, that was what Anna discovered the most. During the long days and quiet nights, she'd taken to reading the Bible with the Brennemans. By their example, she'd soon discovered that it was possible to walk daily with the Lord. And in so doing, she'd discovered a great many things she used to take for granted.

Now she found herself recognizing "God moments" in her life. She found herself enjoying nature more. She found herself valuing all things, not just the activities or items that relieved her boredom or gave her a much-needed jolt of energy and excitement.

"I'll be okay," she said softly to Henry. To her pleasure, he nodded and let her pass.

And, as Anna took that long walk toward Rob and her past, she realized she was, indeed, going to be just fine.

Rob smirked when she joined him in the entryway. "Anna, if I didn't recognize those remarkable eyes of yours, I might've walked right by you."

To her surprise, she no longer feared his words or his hand. "Why are you here?"

He looked nervously about, but Anna wasn't sure if his unease came from the arrival of her parents and the whole Brenneman family, or from her new attitude.

She privately hoped it was her. No longer was she submissive. Cowed. No longer was she blinded by his slick good looks or the promise of a diamond ring. Here, surrounded by all the people she loved, Anna felt different in his company, like she could stand up straighter. Speak with a little more force. She now had an inner core of strength that sustained her like nothing she had recognized in her past.

Ignoring everyone surrounding them, Rob said, "I came for you, Anna. We need to talk."

"Go ahead."

Out came the campaign smile. "Not here. Come home with me and we'll get you back where you belong, out of those ridiculous clothes. I've got a taxi outside waiting."

"I'm not going anywhere with you."

"I didn't come for a visit, Anna. I came to retrieve you, and I'm going to do that." His eyes narrowed. Eyes so magnetic and such a dark gray, she'd once thought she could read his mind, just from one of his smoldering looks.

Now she knew she hadn't read anything truthful. "No, Rob, you're not going to 'retrieve' me."

"Don't cross me. It's been a rough month. I've spent more time and money than I care to say looking for you."

"You shouldn't have wasted your time—or the taxpayers' money. Whatever we had was over. Is over, and has been for quite a while."

"I don't know why you're talking that way."

"You hurt me, Rob."

"I barely touched you."

"Barely" didn't quite describe the bruise on her cheek. It certainly didn't describe the all-encompassing fear she'd felt when she'd first fled her home.

Behind her, Anna heard her mother gasp. But to her great relief, everyone else stayed silent. "You won't ever touch me again."

To Anna's dismay he flashed a campaign smile at everyone assembled. "Listen to you—always the drama queen." He chuckled. "Don't you think we can save the dramatics for the high school plays?" Linking his fingers around her elbow, he caught her firmly. "I'm done here. Let's go, Anna. Now."

"Release her. Now." Her father stepped forward. "Never again will you take her anywhere. We're going to press charges against you, Peterson."

Rob's hand fell limply to his side, but his voice was still strong and sure. "For what? Looking for my girlfriend?"

"For following us. Tapping our phones."

"They won't be able to prove a thing." Like a fickle wind, Rob changed course again. His voice turning slow and seductive, he murmured, "Anna, don't make me beg. Come home with me, sweetheart. You know I need you."

As Anna remembered how she'd once believed him when he'd talked like that, she felt sick. "Oh, Rob. You don't need anyone. You're just afraid of what I could tell people about your campaign contributions. About how you've been misappropriating them. I bet some of your large donors would love to have that leaked out to the press."

Turning confident again, he shook his head. "That's not going to happen."

"You forget, Rob, that I've filed hundreds of your receipts and papers. You thought I wasn't paying attention—that I was too dumb to know what you were doing, but I remember everything."

In a split second, he grabbed her. "Stop. Don't say a word."

"Why? What are you going to do, Rob? Shoot me?" She'd said the words with far more sass and assuredness than she felt inside. Inside, she was shaking like a leaf.

To her surprise, Rob very calmly reached into his suit jacket and pulled out a small—but still very lethal-looking— pistol. Very steadily, he cocked it and held it out for her to see. "I don't want to do this here. But if this is what it takes, I will."

Behind her, Anna heard Irene whimper.

"Don't, Rob. You don't know what you're doing."

His eyes, as dark as charcoal, gleamed. "That's where you're wrong. I know exactly what I'm doing." Deliberately, slowly, he leveled the pistol at her heart. "I always know exactly what I'm doing."

Anna was afraid he did. She was afraid he was so intent on claiming her that he was willing to do anything to achieve his goal. Even bringing a weapon in the Brennemans' house.

Even scaring everyone half to death.

Even shooting her in order to get his way, even if killing her would ruin him forever.

Rob Peterson had won.

"I'll go with you," Anna exclaimed. "Put that down."

"It's too late for that."

"It's never too late. It's never too late to change." With slow movements, she opened the front door and led the way to the porch. The bitterly cold wind greeted them, sliding through the gaps in her pinned dress and burning her skin. Anna almost welcomed the sensation. She'd brought all this upon herself. And though she'd naively hoped differently, her worst nightmare had come true—she had endangered everyone in the house. As the wind whipped her skirts, she started toward the front steps leading down to the walkway and parking lot.

Behind her, Henry said, "No, Anna."

"I'll be fine." She was out of choices. As Rob was demonstrating, it was time to stop living in her dream world. In the world she lived, no one was free to do exactly what they wanted.

Everyone has responsibilities. You couldn't neglect them or run from them. They were part of life. And a necessary part of her life was Rob.

Obviously relieved, Rob wiped his brow. In the twilight, she noticed that his skin was sallow and damp. Lines of strain surrounded his lips.

Now that she was used to Henry's wholesome good looks, Anna wondered how she could have ever been drawn to a man like Rob.

"You know we can't work things out, don't you?" she asked as they descended the short expanse of wooden stairs.

"It doesn't matter. People expect you to be with me. They expect *us*."

"But there is no us. Not any longer."

"There can be again."

"Rob, you need to rethink what you're doing."

"I'm in this too deep, and so are you." He grabbed her elbow, his fingers pressing into her skin, bruising her. "Let's go. I'll coach you in the car."

She wanted him away from the Brennemans, but suddenly Anna knew that if she went in that car with him without a fight, she would be putting herself in jeopardy.

Because no one else had followed them outside, she dared to stand up to him again. "Rob, no matter what you do, I won't stay with you."

"Anna, Anna, Anna. I'm through playing games." He jerked her to him roughly. She fended him off with a blow to the face.

Footsteps clattered along the wooden porch behind them.

To her surprise, Henry grabbed Rob by his left arm and pushed him away, easily showing his strength gained from years of toiling out in the fields. Then, before Rob had a chance to recover, her father whacked Rob on the neck with one of John Brenneman's hand-carved wooden canes that always rested next to the front door.

Rob's head ricocheted back, snapping in surprise.

And then he fell. Unconscious.

It was over.

Chapter 16

"Well that's surely the most unusual use I've ever seen for one of my canes," John Brenneman said as he stood over a knocked-out Rob Peterson. "It surely did a good job on that Englisher's neck, I tell you."

Henry burst out laughing. "Next time we sell them at the farmers market, I might be tempted to share that story a time or two. Those canes are a bit sturdier than they look."

"It's our hardy hickory, I'll tell you that," John said with a laugh.

Actually, all of them shared a good chuckle. It felt good to diffuse the riotous emotion that had taken place during the last fifteen minutes.

With a meaningful look toward Anna, Irene said, "Let's hope and pray we never have a need for such a use of a cane again, John. I don't know if my heart will be able to take another episode like this."

"I know mine can't." Meredith half cried and half laughed as she pulled her into a hug. "Oh, Anna. I think I just about had a heart attack, I was so very worried."

"I felt that way, too," Anna admitted, enjoying the feel of her mother's comforting embrace for the first time in what seemed like ages. "I was so scared."

"You surely didn't act that way," Katie commented, grabbing hold of her hand as well. "You looked as cool as a cucumber, I must say."

As she and her mother pulled away, Anna wiped her brow. "Not anymore. I'm shaking like a leaf."

Her dad looked at her with concern. "But you're all right? He didn't hurt you?"

"I'm all right."

"I'm glad of that," Henry said quietly. "There's a length of rope in my workshop. I'll go fetch it and then tie him up."

Mr. Brenneman nodded. Though Rob looked to be unconscious, the older man firmly placed a hand in the middle of Rob's back. "I'll keep him here until you're ready."

Anna's mother pulled out her cell phone and dialed 911.

Her first instinct was to tell her not to contact the police, but Meredith shook her head. "No more secrets. No more promises of lies. It's time to move forward . . . starting now."

Irene wrapped a comforting arm around Anna, smiling softly. "Anna Metzger, I never would have dreamed I'd say this, but I have to admit I've never been so happy to see such English here. Now your problems are over and we can move on. All of us."

Katie smiled brightly. "You are in hiding no longer. Now you can go back to being your regular self."

So many changes, so many close calls, all having taken

place in practically the blink of an eye. Anna felt dizzy. Sitting down on the bottom step of the house, she did her best to take charge of her emotions. But she knew it would take more than just the will to be tough. Tremors flowed through her body. She really had been afraid that she was going to have to go with Rob.

The taxi!

Looking up, she saw a strange man hovering near the vehicle, a look of distrust and . . . distaste? On his face. "Dad, look over there. The taxi driver's still here."

"I'll go talk to him."

Her father met the taxi driver halfway. "We've called the police. I've also written down your license plate number, so don't even think about skipping out of here."

The driver held up his hands as he approached their small group. "I wasn't planning to do any such thing. Instead, I was coming over to offer my assistance." Together, the driver and her father approached the rest of the group. To all of them, the man said, "My name is Omar. This man paid me a thousand dollars to take him here."

Katie's eyes turned into saucers. "A thousand dollars!"

In a burst of recognition, Anna said, "You took me here, too."

"Just yesterday a sheriff approached me and asked me questions. Next thing I knew, this man ordered me to take him here. I couldn't say no."

"I'm surprised you even remembered me," Anna said. "You have to have several dozen clients a day."

"Yes, but none wanting to go way out here. And not too many, I'm sorry to say, with your green eyes."

Her mother shook her head. "My word!"

Omar shrugged. "He paid me a lot of money, yes. But he also threatened my citizenship. He said he was going to pull my green card if I didn't comply with his orders." With a helpless look toward them all, he shrugged. "I am no match against such an influential man, do you see?"

Anna didn't have to be told what it felt like to be under Rob's thumb. "I do see. I've been there myself."

"He's a bad man."

"He is."

Ever the hostess, Irene came out with a Thermos of hot coffee. Katie followed with a tray of mugs. The little group each filled a cup happily, enjoying how the hot liquid warmed them from the insides.

John tilted his head. "I hear sirens. The police are coming."

Sure enough, the screaming sirens, sounding so overly loud and harsh, filled the air. A few cows in the back pasture mooed their dismay.

And then they all turned, watching as one police car after another filed up the long driveway, followed by an ambulance.

As everyone talked and waited for the emergency personnel to arrive, Anna remained apart.

She felt extremely out of sorts, like she was currently standing in two different worlds.

Though the others looked at her curiously, everyone gave her space. Anna knew they thought she was shaken up from the extreme danger she'd been in. And that was true. When Rob had pulled out the gun, she'd only thought of getting him away from everyone she cared for. She hadn't put herself first at all, until she'd seen that taxi and knew that he was desperate enough to be extremely violent.

But that wasn't the complete reason she was upset. Not by a long shot. Selfishly, internally, she knew the real reason she was miserable—and it was plain and simple: now she would have no reason to stay.

She had to go out into the world again, away from the Brennemans' Bed and Breakfast.

Out of the only place she'd ever truly felt accepted. The irony that she could now leave the only place she'd ever felt as if she truly belonged was almost unbearable.

But like the good friend she was, Katie seemed to know more was going on. As the uniformed officers got out of their squad cars and the men rushed forward to recount the events, Anna walked to the step where Katie was perched.

"After everything that happened, I can't believe things are all over."

"I feel the same way."

Quietly Katie watched the officers. "They'll be speaking with you for some time, I suppose."

"I imagine they will. I'm the reason all this happened."

"Haven't you learned anything yet, Anna? This was meant to happen."

"I certainly don't know why."

"You don't need to. But perhaps you need to remember something?"

"What's that?"

"I've liked having you here with me, Anna Metzger. It's been *wunderbaar gut*. Wonderful good."

Linking her arm through Katie's, Anna smiled. "Yes, it has been. Living here with you has been *wunderbaar schee*." When Katie giggled, Anna scowled. "I know that sounded horrible. But I'm learning and trying, aren't I?"

"You are, indeed," Katie said, just as a female police officer and an EMT approached.

Henry spoke with the authorities, and did his best to see to their needs and answer questions quietly and honestly. Sheriff Tucker, though not a friend, was certainly not a stranger.

Over the years, Henry had had time to visit with the sixty-year-old sheriff, either during community fund-raisers or when there'd been some cases of vandalism at the local Amish school. Their paths had crossed again when a buggy had been hit by an English guest at the inn.

Tucker's eyes widened as soon as he saw who was on the Brennemans' front porch. He took frantic notes as one by one, Anna, Meredith, and Calvin Metzger attempted to relay all that had transpired in the last month.

During all of this, Henry took care to check on Anna, who looked painfully unsure and worried. He was torn between wanting to run to her side and ask her if she still yearned to stay with them, or encourage her to go back among the English, where she most certainly would want to be now that everything was much better.

But instead of talking about any of that, Henry stayed away, giving her space to come to grips with all that had happened. Giving himself time to rethink things and to guard his emotions.

Two hours later, Rob was escorted away in handcuffs by Sheriff Tucker's deputies.

"You all did a fine job apprehending him," Tucker said to Henry's father. "Now I know who to call if I'm ever in need of help during a takedown."

John laughed. "Only if canes are needed, I'm thinking." Turning somber, he said, "To tell the truth, I'd be mighty pleased if nothing like this ever passed my way again."

"I hear you. I'll pass the word if we need you to give another statement, John."

"I'll help how I can."

Tucker looked at Anna. "You'll need to be available for more questioning."

"She'll be at home," Mrs. Metzger said, her tone strong and sure.

Henry felt as if his heart had stopped beating when he saw that Anna didn't look surprised to hear her mother's promise.

Well, there it was . . . she was going. Most likely, never to return, just like Rachel.

Standing in the front yard, looking at her parents, Anna felt a jolt of longing for home. A longing to belong, to be content in her surroundings. The thrust of emotion was so strong, it took her by surprise.

Because she wasn't simply looking forward to the life she once knew, she was yearning for the feeling she'd just learned to accept and look forward to.

That caught her off guard. Had she really become homesick for the Brennemans' home, instead of her own? Where was "home" now?

Suddenly, it didn't seem possible to straddle the two worlds any longer. She was going to need to make a choice, and she was going to need to make it very soon.

But once again, her mother was attempting to do it for her.

"How long is it going to take you to get your things together?" Meredith asked. "It's time we got out of the Brennemans' hair."

She wasn't ready! "Mom, maybe we could wait a while."

"For what? The police said they'll contact us later."

Her mother's rush to be on her way caught Anna off guard. Anna wanted nothing more than just to sit for a while, then attend to her chores and spend some quiet time thinking about everything that had just happened.

Helplessly, Anna looked toward Katie, Henry, and their parents. None of them said a word. She couldn't read their posture, either. Were they anxious for her to get on her way? For her to ask to stay?

Finally Anna caught Katie's eye. Instead of a friendly smile, Katie was worrying her lip. Her blue eyes looked troubled and more than a little shocked, making Anna feel guilty about even wanting to delay her departure. This afternoon's excitement had been difficult, to say the least. The Brennemans probably couldn't wait for her to be on her way!

Perhaps it was time to go. "I could be ready in twenty minutes or so."

"That's fine. Dad and I will see how we can help put things to rights around here."

"All right." Fingering her *kapp*, Anna amended her words. "Actually, it might take me a little longer, now that I think of it. I'm going to need to get my things together." And change. It was time to change into her jeans and sweater and uncover her hair. It was time to go back to how things used to be, whether she was ready or not.

A bit of compassion lit Meredith's eyes. "I understand, dear. I do. Take your time."

"We'll see you when you come back down," her dad added.

Suddenly, Anna knew she needed some alone time or else she would scream. "All right, then. I'll hurry." Afraid to look at the Brennemans again, she started up the stairs, head down.

Like a guardian angel, Katie rushed to her side. "Maybe you don't need to hurry so. Perhaps you could stay the night and then leave in the morning?" She looked at Henry. "That sounds *gut*, don'tcha think?"

"I'm not sure." Henry's face was a mask of emotion. "What is it you want, Anna?"

Before Anna could formulate a reply, her mother answered for her. "It's really time she left. Now. We don't want to impose any more on your hospitality. I'm sure all of you are quite ready to have your guest bedroom free again and get your lives back to normal."

John scratched his graying beard. "Normal? I'm in no hurry for that."

But Calvin Metzger didn't even attempt to catch the joke. "It's time we got her home where she belongs, Mr. Brenneman. You've had to take care of Anna long enough."

Irene looked stunned. "She was a *gut* worker. Wonderful *gut*."

"That's good to hear. At home, sometimes she doesn't follow through on everything she says she is going to." Calvin chuckled. "Maybe this is your calling, Anna. To be in the hospitality industry. That's one of the few occupations you haven't attempted yet."

Her mom snapped her fingers. "That's what we could do, Anna. Get on the Internet and research classes in the hotel industry."

Then, to Anna's shame, her dad reached in his pocket and pulled out his wallet. "Seriously, though, we certainly appreciate everything you've done for Anna. Feeding her, clothing her, making her feel so welcome. Let me pay you for your troubles."

Anna put her hand on her father's arm. "Don't."

"Don't what? Thank them?"

"We already have thanked them."

Turning his back on his daughter, Calvin stepped toward Mr. Brenneman. Anna swallowed a lump, seeing that he was now insulting the family even further by ignoring Mrs. Brenneman, who ran the inn so very competently. "So, John, will a thousand dollars be enough to cover her expenses for a month, give or take?" He pulled out his wallet. "Do you take Visa?"

"We don't wish to be paid."

"She used a room. I don't want to think that she's been taking advantage of you."

"She's been like a daughter to us," Mrs. Brenneman said quietly. "You don't ask your daughter to pay rent, now do you?"

"But—"

"Stop, Dad."

Meredith, her expression stricken, finally entered the conversation. "Let's go sit down and wait. Now."

Anna hung her head as she rushed away. At the moment, she couldn't face any of them. Not John and Irene. Not Katie. Not her parents. And certainly not Henry.

She ran to her room and dug out her suitcase. Inside, neatly folded, were the jeans and sweater she'd worn the afternoon over a month ago.

How could she measure all that had happened? It seemed

a lifetime had passed. More experiences than she could put into words or that she had a feeling she would fully realize in the next few days to come.

She'd entered the inn scared and alone. Not trusting anyone. Now she trusted God and His role in her life. She now believed in herself, and valued her worth. She counted Katie as a sister. Irene and John as treasured mentors.

And she trusted and longed for a future with Henry like no other.

Chapter 17

An early spring storm came unexpectedly, bringing with it a batch of brilliant white snow. It continued on for the next twelve hours, keeping everyone in the region indoors. Just when it looked like a break was in sight, the temperature warmed up enough to turn the powdery flakes to sleet. When the temperature dropped again, the results were truly beautiful. Thick sheets of ice coated everything in sight, casting a lovely, shimmery otherworldly glow over Cincinnati.

Anna wished she was in the state of mind to appreciate the wonder of it all. Instead, all she could do was feel trapped.

Two weeks had passed since the afternoon both her parents and Rob had come to the Brennemans' home. In that time, her feelings had run the whole gamut of emotions, from joy to being free from Rob Peterson's abuse to enjoying the many modern conveniences of home to missing Henry.

Things with her parents were rocky. Her mother either

tried to be too friendly or treated her as if she were eight years old.

Anna had had to visibly bite her tongue when her mother had not only asked where she was going, but with whom and when she'd be back. Anna couldn't blame her. She knew her parents had been worried sick when she'd been gone. Therefore, she tried to be patient and give the information that was asked. But still, the heavy-handed guardianship was uncomfortable and confining.

It felt so different than her life at the Brennemans'. Yes, she'd been subjected to the lifestyle of the Amish, and she'd certainly been often surrounded by other people. But she'd also been given responsibilities and the freedom to explain herself.

Now Anna felt lost and unable to completely apologize for her actions. Quite simply, there were no words to say.

"So, that's how I'm feeling, Julie," Anna said after speaking almost nonstop for the last half hour. "I feel torn between two worlds, which seems really ridiculous because I was only pretending to be in one of them."

"Which world were you pretending to be in?"

That took her by surprise, the answer was so obvious. But, because Julie had never been one to be obvious about anything, Anna asked, "What are you talking about? I was only pretending to be Amish, of course."

Julie pushed the bowl of ice cream away, the mound of vanilla having long turned soupy. "Here goes. I'm going to say something that you might find surprising."

Julie had never been one to beat around the bush, either. "Okay."

"I think maybe you were supposed to be at the Brennemans'.

I think you were meant to live with the Amish and adopt their way of life. I think that's maybe where you are supposed to be. That you fit in with the Amish." Slyly, she added, "And with Henry."

"I think you're mistaken. I didn't fit in with them, not really." Anna couldn't even bring herself to talk about Henry, her feelings toward him were too raw and volatile.

"From what you've told me, you were happy at the inn."

Was that the emotion that came to mind? Anna didn't dare risk analyzing that one. She'd been confused at the bed and breakfast. Confused about how she'd come so far as to be the type of person who had to hide in order to save her sanity. Confused about her feelings for Henry. Confused about how she could trust the Brennemans so much when she didn't trust her parents at all. "If you had seen me there, you'd know I wasn't 'happy.'"

"Content?"

Since when did her best friend ever care about things like contentment? "Julie, you've got it all wrong. I did make the best of the situation I was in. And I did enjoy living with the Brennemans. I loved a lot of things about their lifestyle . . . from the satisfying work they did to the way our evenings were spent playing games or quilting or just talking. But, they were merely being kind. I didn't fit in."

"You really didn't? Or have you become so accustomed to not fitting in that you made up your mind that things weren't going to work out? And that you would never be okay there because you weren't willing to work a little harder?"

Now she was psychoanalyzing her! "Julie, what's going on? You of all people—"

This brought a bright smile to Julie's face. "Me, of all

people? I'm no different than I once was. We've known each other forever. We still like the same books, the same television shows. We can still find humor in the strangest places, and even though we sometimes date real jerks—" Julie let her gaze rest on Anna for a moment while that one sunk in—"we're still willing to go to bat for each other, through thick and thin."

"That's true."

"If it's true, then why are you doubting me?"

Julie's words had merit. Her faith in her was also very humbling. But Julie hadn't lived among the Amish. She didn't really know what she was talking about. She couldn't. Could she?

Or had Anna, too, begun to only judge people on appearances instead of what was inside of them? Of what was in their hearts? "I don't want to argue."

"I don't, either. But I also don't want to be ignored. Listen, Anna. Just because I have tattoos and an earring in my eyebrow doesn't mean I care about you—or the things and people around me—any less. You should know that appearances aren't everything."

"I realize that. I just am having a hard time understanding how you would be on the side of the Amish."

"Because your face lights up when you talk about them. I think you have something special there. Especially with Henry."

Just hearing his name made Anna feel warm. His name brought forth images of walks in the fields. Of quiet conversations on his front porch and in his workroom. Of meaningful discussions and jokes and bright light.

But that didn't mean her attraction was right. "The only

way I could have a relationship with Henry Brenneman is if I became Amish. And that decision would be have to be for life. He's been hurt before. The woman he was courting left him for an Englisher. I couldn't bear to hurt him as well."

"Then don't."

"But the only alternative would be to join the order. To become Plain."

"And your problem is—"

Anna stood up in a temper. "Julie, I can't become Amish!"

"Why not? You already were."

"That was just pretend."

"Was it?"

Julie's question, offered so calmly, took the heat from her anger and replaced it with a quiet circumspection. She sat back down. "Truthfully, when I was with the Brennemans, nothing was fake. I felt genuine for the very first time. Honest, stripped of all the layers of coverings I've adopted in order to survive in the 'real' world."

"Would Henry say that he lived in the 'real' world?"

Anna didn't hesitate over her answer. "He'd say that his world was far more real than the outside one."

"I thought you believed in Jesus Christ."

"I do," Anna protested, still thinking it was an odd conversation with Julie. "Do you?"

"I do."

"But the tattoos . . ."

She laughed. "I'm not perfect. I do like to express my personality in the way I see fit. This look of mine fits my lifestyle. But like your friend Henry or Katie, I'm not letting other people's perspectives on my outward appearance affect what is in my soul. Of course, I'm not trying to be Amish, Anna. I'm just trying to be myself."

What Julie said made a lot of sense. And that straight talk also encouraged her to dive into her insecurities. Admitting the one closest to her heart, she said, "I don't know if Henry would even want me."

"Maybe you should ask."

"I can't. They don't have a telephone, and there's no way I'm going to go show up on their doorstep again, uninvited." Just the thought of doing that again scared her half to death. Katie would most likely think she was on the run again!

Still on target, Julie said, "Could you write to him? Tell him how you feel?"

"I could. I mean, I guess I could. But what if he never answers?"

"That would be tough. But would it be any tougher if you never did a thing and your Henry thought you never cared?"

If Henry did feel as invested as she did, Anna was very afraid that her leaving him would hurt him deeply. She couldn't do that.

She knew then that it was time to trust herself and take a step forward in claiming her life. In following God's path and walking toward the life she really felt she was meant to lead.

"All right, I'm scared to death, but I'm going to do it. I'm going to write to Henry. I'm going to be honest and open and tell him how I feel."

"Good girl. And what are you going to do if he feels the same way that you do?"

Anna couldn't help but smile. She loved how Julie wasn't looking for the negatives but the positives. "If he feels the same way, I guess I'll need to go speak with his family. And mine." But in the end, Anna knew, she was going to depend on herself and not on what others expected of her. She was finally ready to be her own person.

Julie grinned, too. "I can't wait to tell people about my Amish friend Anna."

"Henry, this came for you today." Katie handed him a letter gingerly, like it was about to burst into flames. "It's from Anna."

Now it was his turn to handle the envelope with care. "It just arrived?"

"*Jah*. It was in the mailbox with today's bills and reservations."

Katie folded her arms over her chest, obviously waiting for him to open the letter and read it out loud to her. But he wasn't about to. There, on the front of the envelope, clear as day, was his name, neatly printed out. It was to him, and him alone.

That had to be a significant thing, for sure.

He fought off the urge to run his fingers over the ink, just to gain a sense of her. Three weeks had never felt so long. Instead, he carefully set the letter on his workbench. "Thank you for delivering it."

Katie folded her arms across her chest. "Well, aren't ya going to open it this minute and share it with me? I've sorely missed Anna. Even seeing her handwriting brings a smile to my face."

He didn't doubt Katie's words, because he felt the same way. But that didn't change the fact that the letter was addressed for his eyes, not hers. "No, I am not."

"But—"

"I'm going to want some privacy when I read it, I'm thinking." He fought against rolling his eyes at his words. Honestly, if Katie had said such a thing, he'd be teasing her mercilessly.

"Privacy?" Her eyes narrowed. "I know you two had some feelings for each other, but I thought that ended when she left. What could Anna have to say to you that she couldn't tell me? For that matter, why do you think she wrote to you at all?"

Henry didn't dare convey the many private talks he and Anna had had during her time with them. It was too personal, and there was too much doubt in them. After all, what, really, could be shared? It wasn't like they'd had an agreement.

Or could ever have an agreement.

"I don't know why she wrote to me, but I intend to find out. Alone."

Katie folded her arms, obviously ready to stand firm. Anxious to read the note in private, Henry resorted to age-old tactics. "You know, you're acting like you used to when Rebekeh still lived at home. Nosy and too willful."

"That's unfair. I was only a teenager then."

"You see what I mean?"

Outside the room, they heard their mother gathering some jars from the storage room nearby. In a huff, he heard Katie call for their mother. *"Mamm,* what do you think of this? Anna wrote to Henry, and he wants to read her note in private."

Henry glared at his sister.

But then their mother saved the day. "I think you are too interested with Henry's business, Katie. Everyone has a right to a private letter." Handing over several of the jars to Katie, their mother added, "Let Henry have some peace now, and help me with these jars."

"But—"

"Katie, I need your help with dinner, and that's a fact."

Henry caught his mother's understanding smile as she motioned for Katie to join her.

Minutes later the barn was empty, save for the animals and Henry. He picked up the letter once again, afraid yet anxious see what Anna had felt she needed to write. Painstakingly, he broke the seal and carefully pulled out the plain sheet of thick white paper.

As he unfolded the paper, he caught the faint, fresh scent of Anna, teasing his memory and making his hands shake.

Once again, he was mighty happy he was by himself.

With a deep breath, he read her note.

Henry,

Please forgive me if this letter is too forward, but I need to tell you my feelings, and I didn't dare visit you without an invitation.

Henry sat down, shock almost blurring the words on the page. Receiving a letter was a big surprise. To read such a thing almost took the wind out of him.

*During these three weeks that have passed, I've
tried to get back to my old way of life, but I keep
getting distracted by something I hear or see that re-
minds me of the Brenneman Bed and Breakfast.*

*I've finally found the strength to be honest with
myself and after many attempts, have finally decided
to share with you my feelings, for better or worse.*

*See, the thing is . . . I miss you and your family.
But even more important, I miss belonging. And I felt
I belonged with you and the Amish.*

*Is that wrong? Have I just completely messed ev-
erything up by being so honest?*

Henry shook his head. No, her feelings weren't wrong, because he'd missed her just as badly.

*Henry, I know we became friends, but I need to know
if you think there's ever a chance that we could become
more. That is, if I became Amish. I mean, if the bishop
and ministers and elders in your order would let me.
If your parents would ever be able to find it in their
hearts to accept me as a suitable wife for you.*

Had Anna Metzger just asked him to marry her?

Henry was so stunned, he now wished he had his whole
family around him. In his memory, he'd never heard of
anyone wanting to join the order. Their way of life was a hard
one to adopt. It would be necessary to learn Pennsylvania
Dutch, as well. Did she realize that? Was she ready?

And—what about all her conveniences? She'd have to give
up her car. That cell phone. Her job.

I know this is forward. And I know I may be set-
ting myself up to be hurt. Or worse, hurt you by em-
barrassing you. And, I don't mean to do that.

But Henry, if you think there is even a possibility
that we could have a future, would you please write
me back?

She signed it simply. Before he even realized what he was
doing, Henry traced her name with his finger. *Anna.*

In a daze, Henry stood up. After walking back to the stalls
and checking on the horses, he made his way back to the
house. Still clutching the letter, he walked into the kitchen.
There, his parents and a morose-looking Katie sat.

All three looked at him expectantly when he joined them
at the table.

"I need all of you," he said without preamble. Pushing forward the letter, he murmured, "As you know, I received a
letter from Anna today."

Katie glared. "Oh, Henry. Tell us something we don't
know, why don'tcha?"

"All right then. Either I have just received the best news of
my life, or the worst." He sat down across from his father and
ever so slowly, pushed Anna's letter forward. "I need your
advice, *Daed.*"

Katie attempted to read the note over her father's shoulder. When he moved it so she couldn't see, she said, "Would
you read it out loud? I'm dying to know what it says!"

"Patience, daughter."

"But if it's good news, I want to know now."

His mother clucked. "Isn't that how things always are with

you, my *liewe* Katie? Be patient. Good or bad, we'll all know soon enough."

The room was silent for a moment as Henry's father carefully read the letter, then without a word, passed the letter onto Irene.

Finally, his mother folded the note and looked at the three of them. "What do you think, Henry?"

"I'm not sure."

Katie glared. "What is going on?"

"Anna wants to become Amish and marry me," Henry finally snapped, his patience at the end.

"Oh!"

His father nodded, though his eyes twinkled with a hint of merriment. "*Jah*, this is mighty important news, Henry. I'd say something this important calls for prayer before discussion."

Henry bent his head and did pray. *Help me, God. Help me know what Your will is. Help me not walk alone.*

Almost instantaneously, Henry realized something he hadn't appreciated for a very long time . . . he never had been alone. The Lord had been guiding him all along.

He had just finally listened.

Chapter 18

Anna didn't have to wait a week to hear back from Henry. In fact, it took only two days.

Anna,

> *I think we need to talk. Would you meet me at the Horse and Plow on Wednesday at suppertime? I'll be there waiting. If you don't come, I'll know you have changed your mind.*

> *Henry*

Suppertime. That would be roughly around five o'clock, when the sun went down and his work in the barn would be over.

Since it was already Monday, she felt a burst of pleasure to know that she'd be seeing him in just two more days.

"Anna? Was that a note from Henry?"

Anna tried not to feel irritated that her mother was in her business once again. After everything that had happened, Anna supposed that her mom had every right to want to cling to her personal life just a little more than she used to.

And because of that, Anna decided to be more forthcoming than she used to, as well. It was time for their relationship to change again . . . this time growing stronger. More real. "Yes." She swallowed. "Henry asked me to meet him for supper on Wednesday."

Slowly Meredith sat down on the corner of Anna's bed. "Why?"

"It's probably because I asked him to consider deepening our relationship." Well, that was putting it mildly!

"I don't understand. Does he want to leave the Amish?"

A second flew by. Two. It was time to tell her the truth, even if it was going to make her mother upset. Even if Henry didn't want her.

Surprisingly, it felt easy. "No, Mom. I am thinking about becoming Amish."

"What?" She shook her head in dismay. "Anna, what in the world am I going to do with you? Just when I think you've grown up, you take on yet another crazy-haired scheme."

Anna struggled to not let her mother see just how badly those words hurt. "This isn't crazy."

"It certainly sounds crazy! Once again, you aren't thinking through things. Haven't you learned anything?"

"Mom, let me explain."

"There's nothing to explain. Now, I held my tongue about Rob, but I'm not going to let you go chase some random Amish boy."

Held her tongue? She'd practically pushed Anna into marriage with Rob! "Henry is not a boy, Mother."

"Well, he's not for you, either. Once you get a job and get back into the swing of things, I know you're going to realize that your time with the Brennemans was just a pleasant experience. But not your real life."

As Anna looked around her room, so full of childish things and past amusements, she knew that she wasn't where she needed to be, either.

Instead of correcting her mother about the "pleasant experience" of hiding from Rob, she concentrated on the future she knew she wanted. "I have done some thinking. And I've been praying for guidance. I've fallen in love with Henry, Mom."

"You were just in love with Rob a few months ago."

The criticism stung, but Anna knew it was no less than she deserved. "Although I wasn't in love with him, I hear what you're saying. But this is different."

"You can't become Amish. We'll never be allowed to see you!"

"The Amish are very family oriented. They would never not let me see you. We'll still be family; I'll just have chosen a different lifestyle."

Meredith picked up Anna's jewelry box, which had been their sixteenth-birthday present to Anna. "You're just going to abandon everything?"

"Mom, I'm not trying to abandon you, I'm trying to finally uncover what has been inside of me all along." Carefully, she pulled the box out of her mother's hand and set it on the dresser. Then she deliberately grasped her mother's hands and spoke slowly.

"Ever since I graduated high school, I've been unsettled and unhappy. For the last six years, I've been trying to fill that void with things and boyfriends and high excitement. But nothing ever felt right. And I tried, Momma. I tried to enjoy college. Tried to think of an occupation that would excite me."

"Life doesn't need to be exciting. One day you'll realize that."

"But life needs to matter, don't you think? Mom, all this time, I couldn't concentrate. And I've been fighting with myself, hoping to make things right. Hoping to fit in."

"You've just dated the wrong men."

"No."

"Your dad and I shouldn't have spoiled you so much. If you weren't running around, expecting the world, you would have had a better time of it."

Anna was disappointed at their conversation. It felt like they were speaking in two different languages. "It's not a man's fault. It's not your fault. I agree that I was spoiled, but I don't think my searching was for selfish, silly reasons."

"Anna, if you could only hear yourself!"

"Mom, I could say the same thing to you. Yes, I chose wrong with Rob. But a lot of other people were also wrong about him! Now that federal charges have been made against him and his campaign is dead, all the truth about him is coming out. He is a very bad and manipulative person. I didn't know who the real Rob Peterson was until it was almost too late."

"So you're refusing to take the blame?"

Anna stood up. Maybe one day they'd be able to be close again, but it obviously wasn't going to happen right away. "Yes. I'm refusing to take *all* the blame for Rob's abuse and stalking of me."

Her mother's face crumbled. "Anna, please listen to me. Maybe you should go on a vacation. Dad and I will pay for you and Julie to take a trip to Florida. A real trip—"

"Stop. Julie's working, Mom. And I can't go to Florida because I'm going to see Henry in two days and plan a future with him."

Tears fell, one after the other. "You're making a mistake."

"I don't think so."

"What am I going to tell your father?"

"Nothing, because I'm going to tell him the same thing I've told you." Softly, she added, "I've been through so much. Enough to know when it's time to follow my heart. Please try and understand."

"I can't."

"Then I'll only ask for your prayers for me."

"You won't like my prayers, because I'm going to pray that you finally come to your senses."

Anna nodded. "May I still stay here until I know what to do?"

"You can. I'd never ask you to leave."

"Thank you."

When her mother stood up and left her bedroom, Anna sat in silence. Looked at the stereo. The closet full of clothes; the vast number of purses and shoes and knickknacks.

Would she miss all of this?

Honestly, yes.

Would giving it all up in order to be with Henry and to feel like she fit in be worth it?

Without a doubt.

The Horse and Plow wasn't very busy. Anna arrived before Henry. After debating whether to wait for him out front or at a booth, she finally decided to go sit down. The temperature was in the low thirties—too cold to sit outside in her SUV.

After much debate, she'd decided to just wear a calf-length denim skirt and a long sleeved top. It wasn't close to looking Plain, but it wasn't overly fancy, either. And the violet color of her shirt made her eyes seem greener, she'd been told.

And though she shouldn't care about such things, Anna knew that she hadn't changed completely. She was still a woman who cared about her looks and wanted the man she loved to think she was pretty.

Then, she forgot all about herself when Henry walked through the door. Once again, she was struck by just how solid he was. Thick muscles and years of healthy food and hard work were evident under his plain white shirt. His cheeks were freshly shaved and the dark hair that skimmed his collar looked damp.

But when his gaze met hers, he looked the same as always— serious and concerned. Honest and fresh. After nodding his hello to the proprietor, he took the chair across from her.

Anna was glad she knew his ways, and the ways of the Amish. Public affection was frowned upon. Actually, drawing any notice was frowned upon. But his lack of exuberance didn't dim her feelings in the slightest.

Actually, his lack of emotion was reassuring, and made her feel like they had something very important and special between them. Secret and meaningful.

"I'm really glad you came," Henry said.

"I am, too. You are looking well."

His cheeks stained red. Anna knew she'd embarrassed him. But when he met her gaze once again, she knew everything was going to be okay. "I'm glad you are pleased to see me. I feel the same way as you. Tell me what's been going on."

His lips curved. "I imagine quite a bit, but I wouldn't know of it. You see . . . I've been focused on a letter I received from a certain lady I know."

There it was: no pussyfooting around. "And?"

"It's concerned me greatly."

Well, that didn't sound good at all. "I see."

The server came and took their order. Anna chose chicken and dumplings with vegetables and a glass of tea. She'd already seen the array of pies on the back counter and was looking forward to a slice of coconut cream pie.

Henry ordered beef stew and hot rolls.

Then, when they were alone again, Anna knew they would once again get to the subject at hand. "I meant what I said in my letter, Henry. I have feelings for you."

"Truly? I'm not just a passing fancy?"

His words stung. Not because he didn't have the right to ask such things, but because they were so close to her mother's harsh questions.

But that's where the differences presented themselves. Henry was obviously laying his feelings out. He was as much at risk to be hurt as she was. With a thoughtfulness she didn't used to possess, she chose her words carefully. "I knew when

I was at your home that there was something between us that was special. I feel a connection toward you that has nothing to do with childish whims or silly crushes. But I don't know if you feel the same toward me. I mean, I wasn't sure of the extent of your feelings."

Their server delivered their food. Both she and Henry bowed their heads to give thanks in silent prayer. Then Henry eagerly dove into his meal. As she saw him eat heartily, she looked at her own bowl. Suddenly, the chicken and dumplings didn't look very appetizing at all.

In fact, at that moment, she was wondering why she'd ever thought she could eat, her stomach was in such knots. Obviously, she'd been too optimistic. Too sure that Henry would still care for her. Too sure that he would want to wait for her to learn the *Ordnung*, the rules of the Amish, and Pennsylvania Dutch.

"Anna, I, too, think we could have a future."

"Really?"

Now he wasn't even trying to hide his amusement. "Yes, *liewi* Anna, dear Anna. I've prayed over our future, and I've spoken to my family about it."

"What did they say? What did Katie say?"

"They were not surprised."

"Really?"

"Really," he said, obviously amused that she kept saying such inane words.

Henry bit into a roll and chewed with relish. Anna, noticing that her stomach was turning hungry again, scooped up a few bites of her chicken dinner and savored how the thick broth warmed her insides.

"They were only hoping you would recognize the differences between pretending to be one of us, and actually—"

"Becoming Amish?" she interjected. "I do. I mean, I think I do."

"We could never marry," he paused as his cheeks colored again. "We could never marry until you adopted our ways."

"I know that."

"Anna, I would do a lot for you, but I cannot change hundreds of years of customs in order to make your life easier. You'd have to learn our language. You'd have to abide by the *Ordnung*. Our way of life is not always easy. The restrictions can be difficult, even for someone who grows up Amish."

"I know that. I didn't come to this decision lightly."

"Then you know that communication with the outside world would be far limited?"

"I know."

"And . . . children?" He swallowed hard. "We Amish have large families. Would you want children?"

"I would want children with you."

"Running an inn can be difficult, and at first we would have to live there with my family, until there was time to build us a home."

"Henry, I know all those things. Why do you insist on reminding me?"

"Because I want you to be sure."

"I am sure." She said the words with as much certainty and power as she possibly could. There were no doubts in her mind, now that she'd seen Henry again, she felt no doubts at all.

"Then what do you see when you look at me and our way of life?"

"I see a future that's secure. I see living with the Lord on a daily basis, not just on Sundays or just when I'm in need. I see being a helpmate to you, Henry."

Inside, Anna yearned to say far more. She wanted to hold him as her husband. To wake each morning by his side, to grow old together.

A spark entered his eyes, but he said nothing, only leaned toward his bowl and ate a few more bites.

Anna contented herself with doing the same. Now that they were speaking of all the things she'd only imagined in the privacy of her room, Anna, too, found the need to have time for reflection.

In short order, their plates were picked up, and Anna ordered a piece of coconut cream pie and a cup of coffee. Henry picked cherry cobbler.

When they finished, Henry carefully paid the check then turned to her. "I know it is mighty cold out, but would you care to go for a short ride? I put extra blankets in the buggy."

Nothing sounded more romantic. She walked by his side to the parking lot, past her own SUV, to where his buggy and Stanley were hitched. Like an old friend, Anna greeted the horse. "Stanley, you look fetching in your winter coat."

Henry's lips twitched as he helped her in, then he even took care to tenderly wrap a thick quilt around her lap.

After settling in next to her, he motioned the horse forward, and down the gravel path, the one that veered from the main road. "I didn't even know this was here."

"It's right lucky it is. It makes traveling at night far better than risking spooking the horses with the passing automobiles."

As minute after minute passed, all the lights from the town faded away until it only seemed like the two of them existed.

The gray skies had cleared, uncovering a twinkling kaleidoscope of stars. The moon had risen and lit their journey. Around them, wind brushed the tall grasses. But inside, Anna had never felt so comforted.

Henry was sitting closer to her than ever before. Their legs brushed against each other's, her shoulder rested against his muscular arm. Though layers of cotton and wool separated them, their chaste contact felt more intimate than anything she had done with former boyfriends in the past.

"Anna, if you would have me, I would like to court you. When you become Amish."

Never had words been so easy to say. "Henry, if you would have me, I would like for you to court me," she replied slowly. Then, with a smile, she added, "When I become Amish."

With an easy motion, Henry directed Stanley to a smooth patch of land off the main road. When they were stopped and no sound could be heard except for Stanley's jangling bridle, Henry tenderly took Anna's hands. "So, your answer is yes?"

She nodded excitedly. "Yes."

Such a look of pure relief and joy entered his expression that Anna felt a jolt race through her. Finally she had a future, a future that felt right and real.

"I'm pleased. My parents would like you to come back to live with us. Katie is eager to help you learn our ways."

"They're not worried about the two of us under the same roof?"

"I'm going to live down the road a-ways, with my aunt and uncle and their family."

She sure didn't want to kick him out of his own home! "Henry—"

He placed one finger to her lips. So gently. "Hush, now. It's what I want, Anna. If you are willing to do so much for me, I can do this, yes?"

"Yes. When . . . when would you like me to move to the inn?"

Slowly he turned to her. "In four days' time? Now that we're together again, I find I don't want days to go by without being able to see you."

She laughed. She'd fallen in love, finally, after all this time. By his actions, she knew Henry felt the same. "I'll be ready. I'll have my dad drop me off."

Henry glanced around them. No one was around for miles. Only the wind and the stars. Very slowly, very deliberately, Henry curved an arm around her and pulled her close.

He smelled like soap and soup. Like horses and cold, crisp snow. Like her future and her present.

Like nothing in her past.

She rested her head against his chest and gazed out into the distance. There, in the reflection of the snow, sat a wild hare. Its body was covered in a speckled fur, but it was out for anyone to see.

"Look," she whispered to Henry, to the man who now meant everything to her . . . who would one day be her husband. "Another rabbit."

He gently rubbed her back. "And this one isn't hiding. He

must have found all he was looking for and is daring to come out into the open."

As the hare ventured out, Anna knew the feeling. There in the winter's night, she was hidden no more. She felt free. Alive. She belonged.

And the moment was so perfect, so right, it was almost overwhelming.

Dear Reader,

Thank you for reading my novel! I hope you enjoyed Anna's story, and that you, like me, fell in love with the Brenneman family.

Writing *Hidden* was a truly gratifying experience. I've loved sharing my faith through writing, and I've also enjoyed getting to spend many of my days writing a story about the Amish.

My days are usually filled with activities similar to any other mom. I take care of my family, volunteer when I'm able, and help organize my two teenagers' and husband's busy lives. I'm in the car a lot, carpooling to sports and church events, and well, anyone who knows me, knows I'm also constantly battling my pile of laundry. I love my family. I love being there for them.

But I'm also truly blessed to be able to spend my days thinking and dreaming about another way of life—one different from my own. An Amish community lives an hour's drive from my town. Over the years, my love of visiting their stores merged into wanting to know more about their way of life. I admire their focus on family and hard work. I appreciate how things move at a slower pace and how many little wonders are appreciated on a daily basis. I'm humbled by their faith. My series, Sisters of the Heart, is the product of my interest.

I have so many people to thank for helping to make this work of fiction happen. My agent, Mary Sue Seymour, who's always believed in my writing abilities. My friend Beth Shriver, whose faith inspires me. My critique group, Heather, Cathy, Julie, and Hilda, who didn't bat an eye when I said I wanted to write a romance about the Amish. My husband, Tom, who is always supportive and has driven me out to the country more times than I can count. But most of all, this book is dedicated to my Bible study group at church. They've given my husband and me a safe place to discover the wonders of Jesus Christ in our lives. Because of them, our lives are far richer.

God bless,

Shelley

Questions for Discussion

1. The concept of what is hidden in a person's heart is a recurring theme throughout the novel. Did one character's "hidden" goals and dreams resonate with you?

2. Another theme in the novel is changed expectations. Is there a time in your life when you've changed course unexpectedly? If so, how has that path taken influenced you in a positive way?

3. Although Anna and Henry were raised in far different situations, they find they have much in common. It is these commonalities that lead them to believe that they can have a future together. What are some commonalities that led you to your significant relationships?

4. Anna is willing to adopt Henry's way of life in order to be with him. Do you think she is making the right decision?

5. Anna soon learns that there is more to being Amish than just dressing Plain. One of the important tenets she adopts is their belief in forgiveness. The book ends with Anna still harboring resentment toward her parents. How should she overcome these feelings? In addition, is Rob worthy of forgiveness?

6. *"Thy will be done."* It is only when the characters put their futures in the Lord's hands that they find joy. When has following God's path brought you success?

7. To this day, the Amish way of life intrigues many. Is there some aspect of their society that interests you?

8. Quilting is an important activity to Anna and Katie in the novel. Her work on the Diamond Square quilt echoes her involvement with the Brenneman household. Is there an activity in your life which not only brings you joy but also provides a connection with friends or family members?

WANTED

**The next book in the Sisters of the Heart series
by Shelley Shepard Gray**

Coming soon from AVON ⚜ INSPIRE

Chapter 1

Katie Brenneman noticed that Jonathan Lundy was crushing the brim of his hat. Round and round he turned it, fingering the black felt as he spoke. Every few moments, without warning, his fingers would clench and the rim would succumb to his grip.

If he continued the process much longer, Jonathan was going to be in dire need of a new hat.

"Katie, are you listening, daughter?"

She started, daring to glance at her mother, who was sitting across from her on the love seat, her current sewing project forgotten in the basket next to her. "Yes, *Mamm*. I'm listening."

"You have hardly looked at our guest once since he's arrived. You haven't spoken more than a few words." Her mother treated Katie to a look she knew well. It said she had better shape up and soon. "Is everything all right?"

Irene Brenneman was a lot of things, but a fool certainly wasn't one of them. Katie swallowed. "Of course."

"Then you are interested in what Jonathan has to say?"

Katie had been fond of Jonathan Lundy for years. She'd always been mighty interested in what he had to say. Not that he realized that. "Yes."

The hat took another beating as Jonathan spoke. "I have something to ask of Katie. Something that I am hoping she would think was a mighty *gut* idea."

Now Katie was all ears. Had Jonathan finally seen her as she wished? As a woman available for courting? Stilling herself, she inhaled.

Her mother's cheeks pinkened. "What was your idea, Jonathan?"

He swallowed uncomfortably. "I'm . . . I'm hopin' Katie—that Katie . . ."

Her mother leaned forward. "Yes?"

"Well, I'm in need of Katie here to help with my daughters."

Her *daed* coughed. "With your daughters?"

Crunch! went the brim again. "*Jah*. Just while my sister Winnie goes to Indiana for a bit."

Katie exhaled swiftly. Well, she'd certainly been mistaken! Jonathan had been thinking of her, but not as a future bride. Oh no. As a nursemaid for his four- and six-year-old daughters.

"How long, again?" her father spoke. Usually he joked around, or whittled one of the many canes on which he was famous for carving intricate designs. Now, though, he only sat solemnly, his expression grave.

"Two months."

Two months of living at Jonathan Lundy's home? Of caring for his daughters as a mother. Of seein' to his household, makin' his meals, cleanin' his home. As a wife would do.

After a long moment of thoughtful silence, her father said, "Two months is a long time, I'm thinkin'."

"I know it."

Oh! Jonathan Lundy still hadn't looked her way! Katie bristled. She hated being talked over like she had nothing to say for herself.

Though she surely didn't like the sound of this conversation, neither. She was about to speak her mind when her mother spoke.

"Mary and Hannah are nice girls, to be sure. And they are a pleasure to be around."

Jonathan nodded. His expression relaxed. For the first time since he'd arrived, the hat hung limply in his hand. "Thank you. Ever since my Sarah died, I've had a time of it, to be sure."

My Sarah. Those words told Katie everything she needed to know. Jonathan might never think of anyone other than Sarah. Ever.

Her mother winced. "Sarah's buggy accident was a tragedy, to be sure. And your sister Winnie and you are raisin' the girls mighty nice, that's a fact." She paused, as if measuring her words. "But, you see, I don't think it would be right for our Katie to take on such a job."

Her father slapped his hands on his thighs. "Not at all. This job you speak of is not the one for Katie."

"If you're worried I would take advantage of her, I promise I will do no such thing. I'll move to the *daadi haus* and be always respectful."

"We are sure you will."

"And I will pay her, too. Please don't think I wanted Katie to work for nothing."

This conversation was getting worse and worse. It was so uncomfortable, Katie no longer minded that they were speaking about her as if she wasn't there.

"Money is not the problem, Jonathan," her mother said sternly.

The decision had been made. Katie didn't know whether to be thankful or disappointed. Here was her opportunity to show Jonathan just what a *gut* mother and wife she could be. Here was her chance! But it was also a chance for Jonathan to only see her as a caregiver for his girls.

And though she'd always wanted to be a wonderful *gut* mother and housewife, she wanted to be valued as *Katie*. As someone special. Perhaps that would never happen in Jonathan's home.

Jonathan looked surprised. "Oh. I see. I was just thinking that you might have an extra hand, now that Anna Metzger is living here."

Katie's father spoke. "Anna is a great help, to be sure. But that isn't the problem."

"What is?"

With a tender look her way, her mother spoke. "It would be improper for Katie to live with you, that way."

"As a babysitter?"

With a hint of censure in her tone, her mother said, "She is a young woman of marriageable age, Jonathan. Certainly you agree?"

For the first time since he'd arrived, Jonathan looked at her hard. From top to bottom. Katie did her best to sit still, chin up, as if she didn't mind being stared at like a horse at market.

Jonathan's hat fell, whether the brim gave out or he was

startled, Katie didn't know. But, he did look mighty flustered. His brow was damp as he reached down to pick the hat up.

The tension in the room increased. Helplessly, Katie turned to her mother. *Say something!* she ordered silently. *Say something to make things better!*

But her mother remained silent. Her father shot her a troubled glance but merely waited for Jonathan to respond.

He finally did . . . very slowly. "Th- . . . though Katie seems . . . Is. Mighty nice—" He shifted. Pulled at his shirt. "I'm not in the market for a new wife, you see."

Irene raised a brow. "Ever? Girls need a mother. Love and marriage is every woman's destiny, don'tcha think?" her mother said gently.

"I don't know about that, to be sure."

Katie felt stung. Had Jonathan become so terribly entrenched in his world of loneliness that he didn't even see that chance of future happiness?

"I've heard enough. I'm sorry, but we canna allow Katie to live there, with you." Her father stood up with a groan. "Now, I best get to work, there's a lot of things that need doing."

"I wish you would reconsider," Jonathan interrupted quickly. "There's really no one else to turn to."

"That may be the case, but honestly, Jonathan, we have Katie to look after. Don'tcha see?"

Jonathan stood up, his expression grim. "I see. I see that I shouldn't have asked for so much."

To Katie's surprise, neither parent refuted Jonathan's words. Instead, her father merely walked him to the door, then followed him outside. Truly ready to tend to his chores.

"I feel sorry for him," she said to her *Mamm*. "Jonathan is a proud man. It had to be difficult to ask for help."

Her mother picked up her sewing again. "We both know pride is a sin, Katie. He will be fine. It is far better if you stay here at home. *Where we can keep a close eye on you.*"

Katie felt her insides come apart. All at once, she knew. She *knew*. Her parents were not concerned with Jonathan's behavior.

They were far more worried about her own.

Obviously they had not forgotten her *rumschpringe*, her running around years, when she'd been rebellious and willful.

No, she'd been far more than that.

Since she'd returned and given her heart to the church, Katie knew she'd been a far different person. A better woman. Obedient. Devout. Helpful. Oh, she'd been trying so hard to repent for her sins. She'd prayed every night for forgiveness.

Katie glanced at her mother again. Her mother's shoulders were stiff, her posture rigid. With great effort, Katie tried to stop her hands from shaking. Had her mother found something out? *Had her mother discovered what she had done?*

"I'm going to go check on Anna," she said, abruptly scurrying from the room.

Miraculously, her mother let her go without a word.

But as Katie rounded the corner and faced the beautiful front staircase, she knew she couldn't face her best friend just then. She didn't want to burden Anna with her troubles, or be surrounded by her joyful nature. Yes, lately, Anna had been very joyful.

She'd had every reason to be. Anna was unofficially courting her brother Henry. She was also in the process of learning everything she could about the Amish and practicing her Pennsylvania Dutch, all in preparation to join their order.

Bypassing the stairs, Katie threw open the door and strode outside, just as quickly as her bare feet could take her.

The late March sunshine brought welcome rays of warmth to the blustery air. Curling her toes into the cool spring grass underfoot, Katie took a moment to quiet down. To remind herself that she was safe.

Just as she closed her eyes to pray for guidance, a fierce yip of a small black-and-white pup caught her attention.

There, at the front of the whitewashed two-story barn sat her brother, a wiggly puppy in his arms.

Katie hurried closer. "Henry, whatever are you doing with that dog?"

His smile was broad and transformed his usual solemn expression. "Caleb Miller's Daisy had a litter. He gave me a pup in exchange for the work I did in his shop last Friday and Saturday."

Unable to help herself, Katie reached out for the pup, then carefully cradled him in her arms. After a bit of squirming, the puppy leaned closer and licked her face. "Oh, he's *wunderbaar schee*—wonderful nice, that's for sure. What are you going to do with him? Is he for Anna?"

"No. She's got enough to do, with the inn and her lessons," he said easily, reminding Katie once again how all obstacles can be overcome with faith and perseverance.

Just a short time ago, her brother took everything seriously and saw little humor in even the silliest of things. His relationship with Anna changed all that.

Now the two of them were entering into a bond that went

beyond all their cultural differences. Each was becoming a stronger person because of it.

"This puppy is for you."

His statement was such a surprise, so wonderful *gut* after the way her fears had once again threatened to get the best of her, tears pricked her eyes. "Truly? Why?"

Looking suddenly bashful, Henry shrugged. "I don't know. Maybe because you love puppies so?"

She was prevented from replying when the puppy wriggled some more and yipped out his own reply.

Henry laughed. "I think the two of you will get along just fine."

"Do *Mamm* and *Daed* know?"

"*Jah*, they know." Scratching the pup on his head, he said, "Don't worry so, Katie. What's meant to be will happen. It always does."

"I hope so." Even though she knew she'd regret scrubbing the stains out later, Katie sat down on the dusty ground to let the pup scamper. He leaped from her lap, sniffed impatiently around the area, then eagerly ran to her again, his tail wagging like they hadn't seen each other in days.

He'd come back to her. He hadn't chased after Henry. Though she knew it was a silly thing to be happy about, Katie was pleased. Perhaps everything did work out the way it was supposed to. Perhaps everything with Jonathan Lundy would work out one way or another, as well.

Perhaps one day, her past would finally stay in the past.

Finding comfort in prayer, she whispered, "Dear Lord, my gracious God, please help me see where my future lies."

* * *

"Anna, you must be careful filling the jars," Katie said gently as she carefully lifted the jar out of the boiling water then poured exactly one cup of preserves into the jar. "If you are not careful, you're going to fill them too full."

Anna pursed her lips. "I thought this was supposed to be an easy job."

"It is."

She held up a finger. "Not for me, I burned myself when the boiling jam got the best of me."

As if he had a radar when Anna was unhappy, Henry entered the roomy kitchen and made a beeline for Anna.

"Anna, you hurt yourself?"

Just like a child, she held up a finger. "It's nothing. Merely a blister."

To Katie's chagrin, her older brother carefully pressed her finger to his lips before leading Anna to the sink. Why was she letting him lead her around? Letting him coddle her? Katie held her patience with effort. No self-respecting Amish woman would fuss over a burn so much.

She was just about to mention that when she realized neither Henry nor Anna would notice if she spoke at all. They were standing in front of the sink, cool water running, lost in each other's eyes.

Suddenly, it was too warm to be there with them. Too confining. Too much.

"I'm going to check on Roman," she said.

Neither looked her way.

Frustrated, Katie ran out to the pen that Henry had made for the puppy. He wiggled with delight when he saw her.

Her mother, out feeding the goats, looked up when Katie

approached. After a moment of careful observation, she spoke as assuredly as she always had. "Katie, you are surely havin' a time of it, aren't you now?"

"I'm all right."

"Come now, I saw you running out here. What is wrong?"

"Nothing."

Her mother nodded to Katie's hand. "Come now, something's wrong. Look what you are doing! We both know you would never pet Gertie without a reason."

That was unfortunately true. Oh, how she'd always hated those silly goats. She had ever since they'd gotten loose one fine spring day and found her quilt on the line. In a matter of minutes, Billie and Gertie had chewed on that quilt, making a mess of years of careful hard work. "Anna and Henry looked like they needed a moment or two of privacy."

"I suppose a courting couple needs a moment or two from time to time." Looking toward the house, she wrinkled her brow. "I thought you were working on jam this morning."

"We are. Well, we were until Anna burned her thumb." Unable to stop the flow of words, Katie let out the feelings she'd kept inside for so long. "Anna's acting so foolish. The way she carried on, you would think her thumb was on fire. Of course Henry came out to see what was the matter."

"He would."

"None of this would have happened if she had been more careful. Anna doesn't listen, *Maam*! I've told her time and again to only fill the jars two-thirds of the way full, but time and again, she ignores my suggestions."

"I doubt she ignores you on purpose. This is all new for her."

"Everything is new. She is helpless."

"She's accomplished in other ways."

"But that hardly matters now. Amish women need to know how to can."

"And she will learn. We all do. The Lord gives guidance, we only have to listen, don'tcha think?"

Now that her temper had calmed, Katie felt embarrassed for her behavior and cross words. Her mother was exactly right. Anna was doing the best that she could, and Katie needed to find the goodness in that, instead of looking for problems and disagreeable things. "I'm sorry."

"I'm not sorry that you're sharing your thoughts with me. Come now, what is really bothering you?"

Katie knew she couldn't pretend any longer. "Anna is getting everything I've wanted."

Her mother's lips twitched. "To burn herself canning?"

"No, of course not." Reluctantly, she mumbled, "Soon Anna will have a husband."

"Ah. You are thinking of Jonathan Lundy and his offer."

"Yes. I want to go to Jonathan's house, *Maam*."

"You'll be setting yourself up for heartache."

"Then let me have heartache while I'm at least trying. My heart already hurts now and I've done nothing."

"I see." After looking at her Katie once again, she picked up her skirts and shook them. "I'll do some more thinking about this. In the meantime, go see to Anna."

"No telling what mess she's made now."

"Thank goodness she has you to clean things up then, yes?"

Katie couldn't think of a suitable reply.

Chapter 2

Some days, Jonathan missed Sarah so much he thought his insides would break.

It was one of those days.

Outside the kitchen, the air was crisp and the sky a beautiful robin's egg blue. Yes, the Lord had blessed them with a perfect late fall day. Within days, the air would become colder and the fields would be covered with a pristine white blanket of snow.

But not quite yet.

When Sarah was alive, she would have been bustling around the house, with every window open to greet the day, regardless of how sharp the wind was. Now he only opened one.

Oh, how he used to grumble about the frostiness of the kitchen. Now, a far different chill permeated the room. One of silence and emptiness. No matter how many people might take up the space, things weren't changing. His wife was gone and in her place was a giant gap of a hole that couldn't seem to be filled.

And he'd tried.

But it was no use. Like a doughnut, there was no center to their lives. The imagery almost made him smile. When Sarah had been alive, he'd taken it for granted that he was the center of the family.

He'd been much mistaken.

Winnie's presence was helping, though lately he'd seen a shadow in her expression. Jonathan knew what the shadow was for—no longer was Winnie able to find comfort in what used to be. At twenty-four, his sister was yearning for a future of her own. A family and home of her own.

Being his lifeline wasn't giving her the satisfaction he'd hoped it would. If he were honest with himself, he knew he should be happy for her. The Lord asked everyone to find a life partner and raise a family. It would be a terrible shame if Winnie did not yearn for those things, too. But oh, how he wished she would have chosen to wait a bit longer for his sake.

Outside the window, a pair of cardinals flew by, the male so proud and bright, his mate far quieter. Yet, together they made a mighty fine pair. Could he fault his sister for wanting what all creatures had?

He could not. But what still remained was his needs. He needed someone to watch his girls while he worked in town for the next four months.

"I canna believe that the Brennemans refused you," Winnie stated over her half-drunk tea. "Your idea was most reasonable."

He'd thought so, too. Carefully, he flipped the eggs in the pan, grimacing as yet again one of the yolks broke and ran across the griddle's surface, hardening in seconds. "Not everyone wants to care for my children, I suppose."

"No, that's not it." She drummed her fingers on the table. "What did they say again?"

"John and Irene said they did not want their daughter living with me. Alone."

"But you would be with the girls." Winnie frowned. "And what is with that nonsense, anyway? Don't they realize that your heart has already been taken?"

It had been, indeed. Jonathan's heart was locked up somewhere else and wasn't going to escape any time in the near future. Most likely, ever.

"Between work and the girls I am busy indeed, but I've a feeling that they don't see it that way."

She joined him at the counter. With easy movements, she wiped off the crumbs of her toast as he pulled his own bread from the confines of the oven. "I should go talk to them. Clear things up."

"Winnie, you mustn't. They've already made up their mind." After shaking a healthy amount of pepper on his eggs and placing his toast on top, Jonathan carried his plate to the table. "Maybe, you could put off your trip for a while."

"Don't ask me to do that. I must go to Indiana. I need to go. Malcolm has been so wonderful *gut* in his letters. There might be something between us." More quietly, she added, "I hope there might be."

He said the obvious. "Indiana is far away." And because he wasn't as good a brother as he wished he were, he added quite peevishly, "They may be quite different there, too."

"Like how?"

"I don't know. But different is different."

She shook her head slightly. "Oh, *bruder.* Sometimes different is *gut.*"

"Sometimes not."

"Jonathan, once you followed your heart. Now it is time for me to do the same."

He knew she was right. Winnie was a pretty girl, to be sure. Thin as a reed, she used to look somewhat like a beanpole. Now, though, she merely looked slender and feminine. Her light blue eyes emphasized her ivory skin and black hair.

Yes, it was time for Winnie to be thinking of courtship and love. "I hear you."

Looking satisfied that she won, she plopped his hot pan in water. "I'll figure something out for you, I promise. I will not go at the expense of Mary and Hannah."

"What are you talking about?" Mary asked, popping her head into the kitchen.

Winnie blushed. "Nothing, child."

"It is something," Mary said in that forthright way of hers. The way that had been Sarah's. Sure, confident. At times— too much so. "I heard my name."

"You shouldn't be eavesdropping, daughter."

Mary crossed her arms over her chest, yet another true imitation of her mother. "I didn't on purpose. But I did hear my name."

Slyly, Winnie raised an eyebrow Jonathan's way. Yes, Mary was a handful, to be sure.

"Your aunt and I were discussing the particulars about our neighbor Katie coming to live with us," Jonathan finally said.

"Why?"

"Because I am going to go to Indiana for a spell." Winnie picked up his plate and rinsed it off. "Would you like an egg this morning, Mary?"

"No. I just want toast."

"Daughter, you should eat more."

As expected, Mary ignored her father. "I don't know Katie Brenneman. Not well."

It didn't escape Jonathan's notice that his daughter wrinkled her nose when she spoke their neighbor's name. "You certainly do too know her."

"I don't see why we want her here. I don't."

All brusque and business, Winnie shooed Mary and little Hannah, who'd just appeared, toward the table. "Sit down, now. It is time to eat."

But the ever-curious Hannah stopped in her tracks. "Who do we not want here?"

"No one," Winnie said as she shuffled Hannah to the broad oak bench.

But Hannah was not to be put off, either. "Who?"

"Katie Brenneman," Mary answered. "And we do not want her here."

Spearing a fork into her egg, Hannah paused. "Why?"

"Because we don't know her," Mary said.

"Well, I do. I like Katie." Smiling sweetly, she said, "Katie gives me cookies at gatherings."

Sounding far older than her years, Mary said, "Cookies do not make for a nice person, Hannah."

"Why not?"

Jonathan could not take any more. "Katie is indeed a nice person, and that is all we will say about that. It is a sin the way you two are gossiping."

"I'm not gossiping and telling tales," Mary retorted, obviously offended.

"Daughters, eat your breakfast and get ready for school. We've had enough talk for now, I think."

While Hannah busied herself with butter and jam, Mary narrowed her eyes. "But—"

"That is enough." As silence filled the room again, Jonathan slipped on his coat and walked outside. Into the crisp, cool air. Into the type of day that Sarah had always enjoyed.

He'd never told her how much he far preferred the hot, long days of summer.

In fact, he'd never told her much about his tastes and wants.

Yet now it was too late.

Shelley Shepard Gray

Photo by Mary Lou Zinsser

Hidden is **SHELLEY SHEPARD GRAY**'s first foray into inspirational fiction. Before writing romances, Shelley lived in Texas and Colorado, where she taught school and earned both her bachelor's and master's degrees in education. She now lives in southern Ohio where she writes full time. Shelley is an active member of her church. She serves on committees, volunteers in the church office, and is part of the Telecare ministry, which calls homebound members on a regular basis.